Who Killed Billie Winters

Book Cover by Stephanie Swann
Formatting by Stephanie Swann
Editing by Beth A. Freely
First edition 2024

Contents

Author Note

This book is many things, but one thing it is not is suitable for anyone under 18. If this is you, please put this down. It'll be here when you're of age.

Rating: R

Contents: miscarriage, murder, death, plot twist that might have you going wtf, motherhood, rural feel, psychological games, hints at DV

Dedication

I wanted to write a book inspired by a song... Darkside by Neoni.

This is that book.

Sometimes the monsters we should fear aren't the ones under our bed

but those lurking outside it.

One

"Hey Billie, wanna get the kids together later for a playdate?" I yelled out my window as I stopped the car on the street. She was plucking weeds from around her cedars and offered a tired smile.

"Sure, Stella, does ten work? I'm just about done with these stupid vines. The more I pull, the more they grow, ya know? Damn pests."

I chuckled, trying to hide my frown. She had bags under her eyes, and her lips were pulled tight. "Sure thing. I'll go get them ready and meet you out here."

As I pulled into the driveway, my heart raced. There was something off about her voice. The strain in her words, the way she gripped the weed puller tightly. I shook my head, dismissing the thoughts. *Jetland must've done something again.* I ushered Max and Garrett out of the car to go play. Our families had been friends for years. Our kids were almost the same age. Garrett and Henley were both twelve; Jennie was nine, and Max was eight. They'd practically grown up together. Billie and I had become fast friends, though her husband had always remained somewhat distant. I figured he was either private or snobby. Tyler and Jetland talked sometimes, but Jet preferred his frat boys to our company, and that did us just fine. We were the kind to enjoy being outside to being in pubs, which seemed to be where Jet laid his hat more often than not.

Max grabbed his scooter, and Garrett pulled his bike from the shed, heading out onto the quiet rural road that led to our houses. We loved living out here; it was peaceful. Quiet. Nothing much ever happened, but it was perfect for country living, without giving up the amenities of getting groceries from the city only a few minutes away.

"Hey Ty, we're just headed out to play with Billie and her kids; we'll be back in later, k?"

My husband grunted in response and went back to fixing the sink. It kept crapping out and leaking all over the floor. Thankfully, he knew what he was doing and was on top of fixing every damn break in this old farmhouse.

Soon enough, her girls came tearing down their driveway with a series of hollers.

"Max! Garrett!" Henley screamed as she rode her bright pink bike in a frenzy. "Let's go to the fields!"

And off they tore. Billie trailed behind as Henley and Jennie raced my boys down the street.

Placing my hand on her shoulder, I didn't miss how she startled before looking up at me, "Sorry, I didn't mean to flinch. Just been a hard day."

"What's going on? Jetland being a dick again?"

"Yeah, kinda. He's just been a lot lately. He's stressed about work. Boss is being a dick, and he's coming home and yelling at me. The girls are having a hard time dealing with it, to be honest. It's... I just hate it. This isn't what I signed up for."

"Billie, you know you can always come to me, right? You and the girls. I've told you that."

She offered me a weak smile. "I know, and I appreciate it. I just... He's not always like this. Or at least, he never used to be."

I glanced over her shoulder towards her front door. The curtains swayed slightly before falling still again. It wasn't that I didn't believe her; it was just that this had been happening more and more lately. She'd been withdrawn. Her eyes were more tired and sad than they were bright and happy. I didn't know how much to ask before she would pull away, and then she would isolate and be alone with just him. As much as Jetland was weird and aloof, he'd never really displayed anything other than cordial pleasantries when we crossed paths.

We fell silent, watching our kids play and tumble around in the long grass, enjoying the sight of their carefree faces.

"You know," she started, "I... I've been thinking a lot lately."

She paused, looking at me quickly before looking down and fiddling with the hem of her shirt. "I think I want a divorce."

I tried to hide my surprise. I hadn't realized things were quite this bad. Reaching out for her hand, I squeezed it gently. "Billie, I'm here for you, y'hear me? You know that, right? Whatever you need, divulging or a shoulder to cry on, I'm here. Tyler would never turn you and your fam away, either. We love you guys. You're like an extension of our family."

She glanced at her house again as if checking to make sure no one was eavesdropping before leaning in closer. "I'm scared, Stella; what if he won't let me go?"

"What do you mean? Like... does he hurt you?"

She didn't need to answer; the way she avoided my gaze said it all. "Billie, fuck. We need to tell someone. We can't let him get away with this."

"No! I can't, Stella! What if he finds out? He'll take my girls away; I know it!"

I wrapped my arms around her shaking body, pulling her close. "Billie, you deserve better than this. You and your girls deserve better than living in fear."

She sighed, watching them for a moment, before her blue eyes found mine, filling with tears. "He hasn't hit me. Yet. Every time I try telling him how his actions affect me, he starts yelling at me. I just want some damn attention. He only cares about going out with his boys, lacrosse, and drinking beer. And don't get me started on soccer. He never makes time for me. With the girls, it's like he's father of the year, but he actually doesn't know a damn thing about what they like or dislike. It's infuriating. I don't even think he remembers their birthdays, quite frankly. You're the only real 'home' I have. The only one who listens. Who loves me."

I frowned. She made it seem like he was beating her, and I was panicked. Ready to call the cops or whisk her out of there. "That's not nice of him. Have you guys gone to therapy or anything?"

She nodded. "Yeah, we have gone for years and years. It's been like this for as long as I can remember. Fuck, Stel. I don't know what to do. I'm losing myself here, and I don't know if I'll be able to find my way back once I'm gone."

"You're not alone, Billie. I'll help you find a lawyer. I'll help you get away from him. Hell, I'll testify on your behalf if I have to. You and your babies don't deserve this."

"Thanks, babe. I... it means a lot to know that someone cares." She smiled gratefully before watching Henley yell at Jennie. "Hey! Hennie! Stop it! Don't scream in your sister's face. That's not nice!"

I bit back a chuckle. Life with kids was insane on the best days, but it constantly felt like we were fielding some disaster. Before we could say anything else, a shadow fell over Billie, and she jumped as if a large hand had fallen on her shoulder.

"I ordered sushi for dinner since you didn't make any, and it's already six."

Billie turned and squinted up into the face of her husband and muttered a thank you before turning back to watch the kids. I didn't miss how she casually shrugged his hand off her body and hunched her shoulders inward.

6'2 to her 5'4, he towered over her with his hands tucked in his pockets. He was handsome; I'd give him that. Jetland Winters was like a walking GQ model with his dark hair and blue eyes. He was always well-dressed and groomed to boot. It was hard to imagine him ever losing his temper or yelling at Billie. But then again, looks can be deceiving. *Right?*

He turned to me. "Stella. How are you? How's Tyler?"

I cleared my throat, frowning as Billie tensed at the mention of my husband's name. "Oh, we're doing great. He's just finishing up a repair. Speaking of the devil, there he is now! Ty! Over here, babe!"

Tyler waved and approached us, engrossing himself in a conversation with Jetland while I mouthed at Billie to meet me for wine later tonight. The conversation died, and Jetland checked his phone, telling Billie dinner was arriving. She nodded once before following her husband inside, yelling at her kids for dinner.

I shuddered despite the warmth of the evening sun prickling my skin. Something was definitely off, but what could I even do about it? She'd been telling me snippets for weeks about what he'd been doing to cause her grief, and I'd chalked it up to marital issues. She'd even said it was because of the moon placement, which was weird, but she didn't seem too concerned until today.

Which is why when she mentioned divorce, it gave me pause.

Was there something much deeper going on that I had missed? Or did people say this when they were frustrated and wanted things to get better?

As I pondered, I rounded up my crew, picking up scattered toys that they'd apparently found in the fields. *Better to collect them now before someone mows over them and shoots them into a window.*

Out of the corner of my eye, something shiny grabbed my attention. Bending down, I picked it up and turned it over in my hand. It was a piece of a mirror. It was almost like one had shattered here, but no other pieces were lying around.

"Hey Ty, do you remember anyone parking here recently? There's a piece of a mirror or something here. Maybe someone hit a car, and they didn't realize it."

He bent down, picked up the piece from my hand, and turned it over, the letters 'obj' visible in the corner. *Yep, it is definitely a piece of a vehicle mirror.* "Nope, I don't remember, but we can check the cams; maybe they picked something up. Remind me later. I'm BBQing tonight. Steak sound good?"

"Oooh, is it steak and BJ day already?" I joked, the kids long out of earshot and heading down our driveway.

His eyebrows shot into his forehead, "No idea, but I'll never say no."

"You make me the perfect steak, and I'll blow your mind."

"Deal."

Two

My phone buzzed against the kitchen counter, interrupting me while making breakfast. Glancing at the screen, I saw Billie's name flash. *Stella, I need to talk. It's Jetland again. Can we meet?*

Of course, babe. Let's have the boys play outside. We can talk then, I typed back quickly, my fingers barely keeping up with the rush of concern flooding through me.

I picked up my coffee, letting the warmth from the mug seep into my palms. "Boys, we're going out to play. Grab your waffles, and let's roll out."

Excited yells filled the house as they grabbed their shoes and stuffed food into their mouths before rushing out the door. It wasn't more than two minutes before my kids were waiting at the end of her driveway, greeting hers as they tore off down the road.

"It's just too much, Stella. I can't handle it anymore," Billie sobbed into her hands, tears streaming down her cheeks.

"Hey, hey... it's okay. Take your time," I said, rubbing her back soothingly. Looking up into her house, I noticed his truck still in the driveway, a ding on the door close to the mirror. Odd, but I couldn't say whether it had been there before or not. I really didn't pay enough attention to stuff like that. "Here, let's go down the road a bit, away from peeping Toms, yeah?"

She nodded and started walking, dabbing at the corner of her eyes. "We got into a huge fight last night. He came home drunk. Again. Lacrosse with the guys all damn day and then decided to go work in the shop instead of helping me put the girls to sleep; he just ignored me when I asked for help. I... I lost my shit and started yelling at him, and then he lost *his* shit. It was insane, Stel, I just... I feel awful. I don't even think he was out playing lacrosse; I think he was seeing that girl again. You remember her? The one he kept saying was just a friend..."

I listened, my heart breaking for her. Billie didn't deserve this, not one bit. They'd been high school sweethearts and were meant to be the perfect couple everyone wanted to emulate: a beautiful house, two kids, and a white picket fence. No one knew what went on behind those closed doors. I knew better than most; I'd consoled her through many a sleepless night over time. "I'm so sorry he did that to you. You didn't deserve it."

She nodded, sniffling into a tissue she grabbed from her purse. "I just... I miss being treated like a Queen, ya know? When we first started dating, he was so sweet and attentive. Now... I don't even know who he is anymore. The only thing that makes sense to me is that he's cheating on me again."

I bit my lip, not sure how to respond to that. Jetland had always been... well, Jetland. But if what she was saying was true, he'd changed since they'd gotten married, as if the ring gave him a right to treat her however he wanted. "I-I'm so sorry, babes. I wish I could say something to help make it better."

She glanced at me, her eyes red from crying. "I know, Stel. I just... I don't know what to do anymore."

"Have you tried talking to anyone else about this?"

"No, who would believe me? He's so charming when he wants to be, and everyone loves him. He's isolated me from everyone!" She spat the last word out like it left a bitter taste in her mouth. "And then there's his damn friends! Ugh. One of his friend's wives is such an asshole! Constantly trying to start shit and ruin what we have. She's a fucking bitch! Walks around like she owns the damn place. He hangs onto her every word as if she knows more than I do, and she fucking doesn't! I bet that's who he's fucking." She spewed, and I raised an eyebrow at the venom in her voice. "I-I shouldn't have said that. It's just..."

"Don't worry about it," I said quickly, patting her arm. "It's okay to vent sometimes. This doesn't go anywhere but between us."

"I know, and I love you so much." She sniffled, then smiled weakly. "You're a lifesaver. I dunno where I'd be without you. Thanks for listening so much lately. I know it's been a lot. It feels like this is all we talk about."

"No worries. Sometimes, we need to get it out; otherwise, it'll eat us alive. What are you up to this weekend?" I tried to change the subject. The truth was, it was getting to be pretty heavy. I was going through a lot of my struggles. Financial stress, work stress. Difficulty with my own boys. I was exhausted and felt alone so often, and with Billie leaning on me so heavily, it felt as if my own struggles were compounding.

The truth was, Tyler and I had been trying for a third baby, and we'd been met with nothing but disappointment. Last week, I'd finally gotten a faint positive, but when I went to get my blood tested to determine how far I was, the doctor told me it was a molar pregnancy and gave me pills to induce a miscarriage. I was struggling and alone. I needed my friend to talk to, but she was going through her own shit, and I felt awful for wanting to burden her with mine.

She heaved a sigh. "Ugh, I don't know. He's just doing whatever he wants, and I'll probably take the girls to my parents. Gets them out of the house. Hey... speaking of. Can you watch the house when I'm not around? I have a weird feeling he's got people spying on me, and I don't have access to our cams. He won't give me user access."

My eyebrows raised. "Oh, of course I can. I'll keep an eye out. We're home all weekend."

Her smile radiated from within. "Thanks, appreciate you. Girls' night soon?"

I nodded. "Yep! Say when."

"Okay, I better head back. Hey Hennie, Jennie! Time to go! Say goodbye to your friends; probably, we will see them tomorrow!"

Their protests brought a smile to my face as they left. "Hey, Mom, do we have to go in?" Garrett yelled.

"No, son, you can keep playing; lunch isn't for a while."

I returned to my front porch to water my flowers before the sun got too hot. Tyler and I had planted this garden when we moved in, and we tended it with love each year. We called it our 'love garden' because it took time and care to keep it weed-free and flourishing. As I grabbed my hose, I noticed the petunias had been stepped on, the petals crushed. A boot print slightly larger than mine was in the dirt, but it looked almost smudged.

I frowned but shrugged it off. Kids, probably. Max wasn't particularly careful of my flowers, and Garrett didn't care at all. They really only enjoyed planting them, but caring for them? Forget it. They both loved the watering aspect, though. The sun beat down on my shoulders, and the sound of their laughter faded as I turned on the tap. A cool breeze rustled the leaves on the nearby maple tree, casting shadows that danced across the porch. It should have been calming, but instead, it creeped me out. All this shit with Billie and her asking me to watch her house was giving me the heebie-jeebies. She must be over-exaggerating. Jet wouldn't have people spying on her. What purpose would that serve?

But what if she wasn't...

I glanced over my shoulder nervously. The neighborhood was tranquil, the only sound being the occasional hum of a lawnmower and my kids' laughter.

Still, I couldn't shake the feeling that someone was also watching me.

Pulling out my phone, I texted Tyler, asking when he was off work, and got an immediate response.

Soon babe. Then we can get the kids into the pool, it's hot as fuck today.

I smiled and sent a smiley and hot emoji before calling the kids to me. I wanted to get into the backyard, away from that feeling chasing me. My phone vibrated again, and I opened it to a screenshot from Billie outlining a long message from her husband. With a sigh, I closed the gate behind my kids and plopped down in the patio chair as they immediately got into the above-ground pool.

Did I even want to read this right now? I was already so emotionally heavy from earlier; I wasn't sure how much more I could take.

"Hey guys, I just need to use the washroom; I'll be right back." I needed to change into something a bit more suitable for swimming and check to make sure I wasn't still heavily bleeding.

As I sat and made sure everything was okay, a wash of sadness passed over me. We wanted this new baby so badly, but one of us wasn't working right. Maybe it was time to see a doctor about some fertility medication. Making a mental note to book an appointment with both my doctor and my counselor to process my grief, I changed into my bathing suit and headed outside to rejoin my kids.

My phone buzzed again, jolting me out of my thoughts.

Stella, what the fuck is this shit? Why is he doing this to me?

A few seconds later, another text came in. I'd completely forgotten to reply to her first message while trying to hold myself together. Shaking my head, I cleared my mind and tried to focus on what she was saying.

Sorry, Stels, you're probably busy with the kids; I don't have anyone else I can talk to.

I shot back a quick response. *No worries, give me a sec, trying to settle them into the pool before I read.*

Oh, thank God. She replied. *I was worried you'd finally had enough. I ... you're like the one person that's helped me be who I really am. Like, I've stopped pretending to be this person I'm not, and it feels like Jet just can't handle that, and he's spiraling into this crazy person, and I can't handle it, you know? All his friends are such losers, and they encourage him to make all these bad decisions. I wouldn't doubt it if that wench was trying to get in his pants. If she hasn't already.*

I responded with a sigh. *Billie, I'm not going anywhere. Vent to me, babe. I got you.* Scrolling up, I read the screenshot from her husband. He was bitching about her not cleaning the house and telling her that he's the breadwinner, and she chose to stay home, and the least she could do was clean and cook. It was pathetic, actually, and I could see why she was so frustrated with him.

Part of his message had been: *I remember we depended on each other when we were young. Now, it's like you don't need me, and I guess I feel like my purpose is gone. Billie, this distance has been eating me alive. I miss my best friend.*

I pondered that before typing back. *Billie, he's spiraling and lashing out because he's insecure about the person you've become. You're not that woman he met anymore, and frankly, that's good for you! You deserve the world, and if he can't see that, then fuck him, is what I say. You deserve better than these mind games bullshit that he is feeding you.*

A simple smiley face with hearts for eyes was sent from her end, and I felt a bit better. I had said some harsh words, but they needed to be said. Jetland needed to realize how good he had it until it was too damn late, and she found a man who appreciated her more. Granted, I only knew parts of what was happening. For whatever reason, Billie never really told me the whole story, and I had a feeling there was more, a lot more, to this than she was disclosing, but I was her girl for life. That's what I did. I had her back.

The sun burned us to a crisp when I finally looked up from my phone to check on my kids. Max had gotten popsicle juice all over himself, and Garrett was on his second. With a sigh, I stood and stretched, calling them out of the pool for lunch. Not that they'd be hungry now that they'd filled themselves with treats, but it was summer, so who really gave a fuck.

I sure didn't.

Three

I woke up with night sweats. Glancing at my clock, the time glared at me—three a.m. My throat was parched, so I walked to the kitchen to grab a glass of water and looked across the street. The Winters' living room light was on, and Billie was waving her hands furiously. Jetland was leaning against a wall, an exasperated look on his face before it twisted into a scowl. I could probably lip-read from here but couldn't find my glasses.

It was wrong to snoop. I knew it. But this whole thing was tearing me up. I was her sole confidante, and she dumped on me almost daily. It was starting to affect my own marriage. To the point that the friction between Tyler and I was growing, and I had nowhere to turn. Half the time that he was ready for us to be intimate, I was too drained. Then, the frustration boiled over, and we argued. Most of my friends were busy raising kids, and I didn't want to burden them. With a sigh, I poured a glass, sipping slowly as I watched Billie pick up a thick book and hurl it at Jetland's head.

That's when he snapped. His whole demeanor shifted, and he stalked toward her, shoving his finger in her face and pointing at the door. She pushed him backward, running past him. He moved to follow but melted onto the couch, his head in his hands.

What the fuck was that? Should I call the cops? Technically, he didn't hit her, so what the hell would I say?

Goddamnit, this was getting out of control. Arms wrapped around my middle; I jumped before Tyler shushed me and kissed my head.

"What are you doing up, babe? Did you have a nightmare?"

"No, just- Billie and Jet."

"Oh Christ," he muttered. "Busy mind, huh?"

I nodded before resting my head on his chest. "It's like a train wreck, and I can't stop watching."

"I know, but you have to for your sanity and mine. I miss you, baby. You've become so withdrawn." His arms tightened around me, and I knew he was right. I had to stop. It was hard when they lived across the street, but I had to try for my sanity. Maybe I'd tell Billie I wanted the friendship to be more balanced tomorrow. I felt selfish even thinking that, with everything she was going through, but I was going through some of my own trenches and felt alone. Sure, mine weren't as deep as hers, but it was like whenever she saw me, I was the dumping ground of trauma, and it was getting hard to separate our lives.

"I'm sorry this feels like it's overtaken our life, babe. I love you. I'll talk to her tomorrow, okay?" I turned and kissed him.

"I love you, too."

With that, I trudged back to bed, closing my eyes and willing myself to fall asleep.

***

I woke the following day to incessant buzzing and my phone falling off my nightstand. Tyler groaned and rolled over, irritated at the intrusion. Leaning off the bed, I picked up my cell and began to scroll through the messages.

I think he's got borderline personality, or he's narcissistic, Stella. I couldn't sleep at all. Honestly, he fits the criteria, which is why I've become who I am. After years of gaslighting, years of emotional abuse, and finally seeing the extent of the damage, I snapped. It's been a long time coming, but I think I'm going to ask him to leave this time.

For good.

I read the messages, and before I could reply, another popped up.

Let's do girl's night tonight. I need to drink some wine and let loose. Fuck him. He can deal with the kids.

Unsure how to feel, I typed back, *sounds good*, before closing the messages, my heart in turmoil.

I hope she knows what she's doing. This seemed sudden to me, but I didn't know the inner workings of their marriage or how long this had been going on. I did know that women hid the extent of their abuse for years before finally opening up enough to let someone see the truth. Memories of last night flooded my mind, and I couldn't stop mulling over what had happened and what she sent me this morning as I stepped into the shower.

"Hey babe," Tyler rasped as he stepped into the small space. I whirled around, and he threw his hands up. "Hey, it's okay; the kids are watching YouTube and having breakfast. Thought I'd join you and see how you're doing after last night."

I sighed. I really didn't want to talk about it anymore. This was now a constant in my life, and it was wearing me down. "I'm fine, baby, really. I'm fine. I want to make sure we're okay. How are you? Feels like I haven't asked in weeks."

He chuckled and grabbed the shampoo, lathering his beard and bald head before handing me the bottle. "Well, that's probably because you haven't. But it's alright. I get it. You're worried about your friend. It's a lot to try and swallow, and it's stressful. I'm okay. A bit stressed because shit at work has gotten wild. I don't know how long they'll keep me, to be honest. Management has gotten out of control, drunk on power, and I am concerned. Stels, we need to start thinking of alternate options."

Alternate options? "What do you mean, baby?"

He sighed, his muscles tense as my soapy hands worked his knots while I let the shampoo sit in my hair. "I don't know, but I have a feeling in my bones. I've been here 12 years and never felt this uneasy, okay? I love you, but I don't think I can continue on this path if they keep this up. I just feel like they're tightening the rope on me, and I can't keep busting my ass for them when they're just so damn ungrateful. I work harder than everyone there, and I still get the shit end of the stick. I've started applying at other places, but we get such good healthcare I don't know if it's wise to move now. I could use some of your wisdom, babe. Especially with us trying for the baby... we might need that healthcare sooner rather than later."

I remained silent as he rinsed and stepped out of the shower, grabbing a towel from the rack. I washed off quickly before stepping out and wrapping my hair in a towel. "Is it that bad that you're looking at other places?"

He sighed before pulling me to his chest, our gazes locked through the foggy mirror. "I don't know, lovebug. I really don't. I just... I don't know if I can deal with this pressure for much longer."

I turned in his arms and looked up at him through blurry eyes. What the fuck was happening? Squeezing my eyes shut against the tears, I burrowed my face into his chest and inhaled deeply. The familiar scent of cedarwood calmed me enough to say the words I never thought I would say aloud. "What about moving? Like... far away?"

He stilled before hugging me tighter. "Yeah," he murmured into my damp hair. "Yeah, maybe it's time we consider a big change. There's a lot of work up north. We can chat more about it tonight."

I tried to smile, though it was more of a grimace, as he pulled on his clothes and stepped out of the bathroom. My phone buzzed again.

Street walk?

I sighed, listening to my kids roughhousing in the living room and Tyler running after them.

Sure, the kids need to get out some of this damn energy, lol!

Wrapping the towel tight, I walked to our bedroom and grabbed some leggings and a spaghetti strap. I needed to talk to her about this. How did I do that in a way that came from a place of love and care while continuing to hold space for her but also asking that she hold space for me?

For some reason, it felt as if she wouldn't be able to do that. Or that she wouldn't understand. Despite being friends for years and almost all of our friendship being smooth sailing, it felt like she wouldn't want me 'stealing her spotlight.' I didn't know why, but an unsettled feeling crept through my body and landed straight in my gut. Swirling and whirling until I wanted to puke. I shouldn't feel this way about asking a friend to meet my needs, too.

So then, why couldn't I shake this feeling that she would freak out on me and shut down?

Grimacing, I tried to clear the feeling of unease and made my way to the kitchen. Maybe some coffee would chase away this ridiculousness that had taken up residence in my mind.

"Mom," Garrett said, impatiently tapping his foot on the floor," are we going out to play with Henley today?"

Ruffling his hair, I nodded, "Sure are, bud. Go get your socks on and help your brother with his and as soon as I'm done with this cup, we will go wait for them, k?"

Their excited squeals and stomping down the hall, coupled with their banter, were music to my ears. I loved being a mom. I loved my babies. Despite everything else, my boys were my entire world, and I would never do anything to jeopardize that. If Tyler lost his job, I'd do anything to ensure the boys were cared for. Even if it meant I stopped being a stay-at-home mom and went back to work. He could stay home. *Hmm... now there's a thought.* I filed that in the back of my mind to talk to him about later.

Finishing off my coffee, I texted Billie.

Front lawn in 5 mins?

She replied immediately.

Yup.

It was showtime.

Four

The kids played fine. It was Billie I was concerned about. She seemed awfully joyful for someone who had a massive fight with her husband and then told me she wanted him to leave. It just felt off. She was all done up with a big red ribbon tying her hair out of her face.

"Yeah, so I don't know," she continued. I'd zoned out for a bit, thinking about the baby, I'd never get to hold. I wanted to talk to her about being a better friend, but it didn't seem like the right time. "Jetland is just so clueless. He plops down on the couch and ignores us all day. I just... can't do it anymore, you know?"

I glanced at her, her hand shielding her eyes from the sun while she shouted at Jennie to stop hitting the cat. I didn't know what to say. This was a complete 180 from a couple of days ago when she had bags under her eyes. Maybe her decision was bringing her peace? *Ugh. Why couldn't I figure out what the hell was going on?*

"Yeah, I get it. Relationships are hard, but are you sure that's the right decision?"

"It is. I have been talking to my grandparents, and they're willing to front the money for divorce lawyers, but you know, here we have to be separated for three months before we can even apply for divorce, which is so dumb because I want it done."

My brows furrowed. "But you haven't even kicked him out yet?"

She smiled. "Not yet, but I will when things are better lined up. Wanna do wine tonight? He's out at soccer and once the kids are in bed I'll dump night chores on him and we can wine out."

"Mmmm, okay." *That might be nice. Get her out of her head, and maybe we can go back to having fun like we used to. Chatting and bullshitting.*

Before all the dark clouds.

"Great! It's a date."

"I... I've been struggling lately, a lot actually. Tyler and I—" I started, but clamped my mouth shut when she glanced at her phone, a frown on her face. "Everything okay?"

"Yep, just Jet again. Ridiculous."

I forced a smile, "Well, it'll be over soon enough..."

She yelled for her kids, "Yeah, yeah, soon enough."

"Okay, well, we should call it a day; I have to get home and start dinner. You know how my husband can be about his meatloaf." I tried to joke, slapping her on her back as she rolled her eyes and gathered her things.

"I'll text you later, but don't forget!"

Max and Garrett dumped their bikes into the driveway before running inside. My mind wouldn't stop turning. Billie was too... chipper, particularly after what I saw last night. If I hadn't seen her throw that book with my eyes and someone had told me, I'd have never believed them. Billie wasn't the type. She was sweet and kind... and what the fuck happened to therapy and communicating? Wine night would be great, but only if she actually showed up as herself and not this Stepford Wife version of herself she was hiding behind lately. Was she seeing someone else? Maybe I can ask tonight...

"Hey babe, I'll get dinner going if you wanna tell the boys to go shower. They're super dirty." I smiled as Tyler walked into the kitchen. He kissed me before going off and dealing with the kids.

Pulling out some meatballs, I got going on a simple spaghetti. Meatloaf would be good, but I didn't feel like making it from scratch.

Wine might loosen her lips enough to tell me what was really going on. Not that her marriage was really any of my business, but I deserved to know since she dumped everything on me and then went about her merry way.

The sound of the shower starting brought me out of my thoughts as Tyler wrapped his arms around me. "Smells delish, babe. Can't wait."

"Hmm? Me too." I shook my butt on his junk. "I'm going to have some wine with Billie tonight, but after..."

He grinned. "Oh, it's on like Donkey Kong."

***

The boys were asleep, and eight rolled around, Billie skipping down her driveway. I'd gotten the wine and a blanket and was excited. It had been forever since we just let loose.

"Hey, you! I missed this!" I hugged her tightly, her body tenser than usual, but chalked it up to nerves. She'd been mood-swinging, and I tried my best to be understanding.

"I missed it, too." She said, eyes flicking to the house and back to me. "Shall we?"

I raised my bag of snacks in agreement, and we went to my backyard, where prying eyes wouldn't see us.

"So, how's things?" I asked, sipping at my wine as we settled under the stars.

"Eh, neither here nor there. I've shut off a lot of my emotions. I want to fix things one minute, and I'm just done the next. I just feel bad if I tell him to leave because of the girls. I don't know if I can do this alone."

I sighed, topping her glass as I turned on some music. "I get it, babe. Maybe just let it go for tonight; decide when you have more clarity; for now, let's do some karaoke and have fun."

We laughed and sang at the top of our lungs. Eventually, we were too tipsy to really figure out which way was up and which was down. Billie lay a blanket on the grass, and we quieted, just lying there, looking up at the stars. There was nothing left to be said; we just enjoyed the quiet for quite a while.

I don't really remember who started it. Her hand brushed mine, and she turned to face me. I rolled over and looked at her, wondering what was on her mind. She opened her mouth, closing it before a blush spread over her cheeks. Then, our lips were locked, and our hands roamed each other's bodies. It all happened so fast. She bit down on my lip, pulling it before crashing her mouth on mine, her tongue playing with mine. Her hand slipped up my shirt; mine fluttered across her stomach instinctually before suddenly breaking apart, her pupils blown wide. Her eyes were locked on my lips, and her cheeks were rosy. She bit at her lip, about to lean forward again, but then she leaned back, scrambling to sit at the edge of the blanket.

"Oh my God. Stella, we can't. I know you and Tyler are open, but I'm not. Holy shit, what the hell just happened? What did we do? I... I don't know what to think right now."

My mind slowed as I tried to process what just happened. One minute, we were singing karaoke, and the next, we were kissing... how did we get here? As I was trying to figure it out, she panicked. Her voice was squeaking as she repeated herself repeatedly, almost in a mantra, "What the hell did we do?"

What was the big deal? She was leaving Jetland anyway. She'd spent weeks telling me that she was leaving him, planning lawyers, how to deal with the kids, what to say. Therapists.

Now, she was going off the rails, and I couldn't keep up with her thoughts. I tuned out her voice while I thought about the right course of action. It was a moment in time. She'd said that the last decade had been a nightmare, and she couldn't escape it once they had Henley. People always left their spouses and did things like this without being formally divorced. I didn't understand why she was so worried.

I held up my hands and calmed her. "Billie, look, I don't know what happened there, but obviously, you were just looking for connection, and I felt safe. It's okay. Just take a breath."

"I'm not telling him. I can't. Oh my God, do you want me to leave him for you?"

I struggled not to laugh. "No, dude, what the fuck? It was a kiss, calm down. Nothing has ever happened before, and certainly won't from here unless you fix your relationship and open it or divorce him and want it to. Tyler won't care."

She had no words. We sat silently for a few minutes before she sighed, "Yeah, you're right. It's... we are just too drunk. You're right. We're fine. I'm gonna go home and sleep, okay? Chat in the morning." She went to stand and stumbled, catching herself before her gaze dropped to my chest and slowly flickered over my lips before she shook her head and dusted her shirt. "Right."

"Sure. Sounds good." She grabbed the blanket she'd brought and left.

I looked up at the stars.

What the fuck just happened?

Tyler wouldn't care; I was telling the truth. We had our own relationship boundaries, and while we weren't fully poly, we weren't entirely monogamous either. I was just more confused as to her reaction. She had leaned in. Then acted like she got burned. Like she was fighting herself, almost. But why?

Maybe she just needed to sleep it off, and we'd chat in the morning. Heaving a sigh, I grabbed the empty bottle of wine and put it in the recycling before crawling into bed beside my husband.

***

The sun streamed through the bottom of the semi-black-out curtains, burning my eyes as my phone vibrated. I checked it, and the memories from last night rushed in. Damnit, we gotta address the elephant in the room.

"Hey, babe?" I nuzzled into Ty's back.

He grunted and rolled over, brushing the hair out of my eyes.

"I kissed Billie last night. Well, she kissed me. We kind of just kissed each other."

His eyes flew open, and he chuckled, "Did you now? Naughty girl."

"Yeah, yeah. She got all weird after. She said something about wanting me to leave you or asking if I was thinking about that, and then she freaked out and left. It was super weird. What do you think about that?"

"Well, I mean, I don't care that you guys kissed, obviously, but yeah, that's kinda odd. Do you think maybe she just felt off-guard that it happened? You guys must have been pretty wasted for that since it's never happened before." He kissed my forehead and sat up, pulling me into his arms.

I nodded into his chest, "Yeah, we were. That's the weird thing. We were having so much fun, and then it just happened, and I didn't really think anything of it, and she clearly did. So, I think I have to talk to her about it. I know I said I would put her drama behind me and refocus on us, but I don't want to leave things unsaid. She's going through a lot, and I don't want to add to her stress, you know?"

He sighed, "Of course not. I fully agree with you. But after this... please, babe. Come back to me. You've been run off your mind about all of their shit, and I've been sorely missing connecting with you. It's been a constant source of stress for you, and I can see it's eating you alive. You're an incredible friend, you really are, but you deserve someone to also pour into your cup, and if she can't do that, you need to take a step back for a while. Plus, we can't really make another baby if you're not an active participant."

"I know... I know. It's just hard. I'm all she's got, and I feel guilty knowing Jet abuses her and she has no one else. But I will, okay? I'll talk to her, and then I'll cool it with all her stuff, and we can go on a date or something..." I pulled away and wiggled my eyebrows. "Maybe you can wear that button-up shirt I like and stash the mask in the back... we can take a drive up the mountain..."

"Oh baby, now you're talking." He smacked my ass as I crawled out of bed, hearing the kids tearing out of their room and down the hall, signaling the start of our day.

"I'm gonna see if she wants to meet outside, okay? Just neutral ground; go for a walk."

"Yep, perfect. I'll be around if you need me.

Walking to the bathroom to brush my teeth and brush my hair, I messaged her to see if she wanted to go for a walk. Her reply was immediate.

Be out in 5.

I got the boys ready, and we went out.

Much to my surprise, she looked happier than she had in weeks and came in to hug me. I side-eyed her as we walked.

"You wanna talk about it?"

She laughed, "Actually, I've done a lot of thinking this morning. I totally overreacted. Honestly, it was nice. I needed to feel loved."

"So... it was just like, you needed connection? Sorry, I'm just trying to understand how you went from being so upset last night to totally fine today."

"Basically. I love you and don't want to lose our friendship, but really I'm okay. I'm not going to tell him because, honestly, he did this to himself. He neglected me for so long that he made me not want anything to do with him. I don't regret anything if that's what you're worried about. I just feel... good. Really good, actually. If anything, I know for a damn fact he's not the one for me. Who knows, maybe I'll switch teams." She pretended to hold a bat and hit a home run before bursting out into laughter.

I breathed a sigh of relief. "Damn, I'm glad to hear that. I mean, I wasn't worried about that; I was worried about you."

She giggled, "Honestly, I'm good. Better than I have been in a while. It was a drunk moment; we are good."

We continued our walk together in a comfortable silence; both lost in our own thoughts before I spoke again. "If you ever want to talk about it, know I'm always open to chatting."

"I know, Stella, and I love you for that, but I kind of just feel like it's a non-issue, you know? In the grand scheme, it's so small, and it doesn't really matter. You are such a good friend to me, which is why I unmasked and allowed myself to become so strong and confident. Confident enough to tell Jetland that I can't settle for this behavior. To tell him I hated his friends and thought they were awful. I've gained so much from having you in my life that I just don't feel like this is a big deal. It kind of felt... natural. Normal, even. Like I could maybe do it again..." She trailed off, and the admission seemed to stun even her.

We stopped walking, and I looked at her, really assessing her to see if she was lying. All I saw was genuine honesty. She really had been feeling alone, and this was just a way for her to reconnect with another human.

"Okay, well, I'm happy if you're happy. But, yeah... I think of you as a bestie and feel like you have to sort out your emotional stuff before even thinking about doing that again." I didn't know what else to say. I didn't really think of her in that way, and maybe it was a tongue-in-cheek comment, but I wanted her to know that I wasn't going to make any moves on her or anything.

"Thanks, Stella." Her smile faltered briefly before she hugged me, and everything felt right, almost like she was back to her normal self.

I paused momentarily, "Hey, can I talk to you about something?" It was now or never, get all the cards on the table.

"Mhmm."

"I've been struggling a lot with Tyler... we've been so distant lately. We're really struggling to connect ourselves. I don't even know how to begin being intimate with him anymore. He's gorgeous and sweet, but it just feels like the longer it goes, the worse the rift gets. I'm always so tired from the kids..." I drifted off as I watched her play on her phone. I wanted to tell her about losing the baby, about the black hole in my chest from yet another loss, but she wasn't listening. "Bills? Are you listening to me?"

She kept typing, a small smile tugging at the corner of her mouth.

"Billie!"

"Oh my God, I'm so sorry! I got a message, and I had to reply. What were you saying?"

I shook my head. Deflated. I don't know why I bothered. "Nothing. It's fine." My lips thinned, and I tried to force a smile. "Who messaged?"

"Actually, if I'm being honest…"

A knot of dread twisted in my stomach as I waited for her to continue.

"I've been thinking a ton about Steve. He was my first love; did you know that?"

Steve. Of course. I breathed a sigh of relief—our neighbor. I did know that he was her first… well, everything. I had no idea that she was still pining after him. She'd told me that she had messaged him a while back, and Jetland had gone through her phone, found the messages, and freaked at her. But I thought after that, everything was done and dusted.

She sighed wistfully. "I just think it would be so nice to have him talk to me while we have wine and just… feel wanted again. Feel beautiful. He was always so good at that. But you know, if Jetland ever found out, he'd lose his shit. Like, I know Steve still wants me. He always has. If you've ever seen how he looks at me, it's obvious."

"Well… are you leaving Jetland or not? Because if you are, then what do you have to lose?"

"Yeah, I am…"

"Well, then, I don't really see anything wrong with messaging Steve and having some wine once you've dealt with all this shit with Jet."

She looked surprised at my response. "Really? You think I should?"

"I mean, I don't think any which way, but I think you deserve to be happy."

Her eyes were unfocused as if she were daydreaming about Steve.

"Thanks, babe. I think... once I figure out how I'm kicking out Jet, I'll send him a message."

Smiling at her, I kept walking towards my sons. They were digging in the dirt, trying to get to a bug. We watched for a while before she clapped her hands.

"Alright, girls, let's go have some lunch. We will come out to play later. Daddy is installing some new shelves and I know you wanted to help!"

She was practically bouncing as they waved and walked up their driveway.

What the actual fuck was going on?

Five

I kicked him out, Stels. Last night. Aren't you proud of me?

The notification was sitting on my screen a week later. A whole, uneventful week passed with more of the same. Tyler and I were working on ourselves, and bit by bit, I began to distance myself mentally from Billie's issues. I was still there for her, but I'd promised my husband I wouldn't let it consume me anymore, and true to my word, I'd done my best.

Yet every day was more of the same with her. Trauma dumping about how horrible Jetland was treating her and me just listening and reassuring her. I was surprised she hadn't kicked him out sooner, to be honest. The kids had no idea what was happening, always just playing like their best friends.

Proud. What an odd word choice. No, I wasn't proud. But I wasn't... not proud?

Using my thumb to open my phone, I replied:

What happened?

Little dots appeared and disappeared before staying around as she typed.

We had a massive argument. He called me a cunt because I screamed at him. Told him he's a sack of shit and a waste of air. I had a meltdown. I couldn't handle it. He tried to make a move on me last night, and I just wanted to vomit. I tried, I tried so fucking hard to make this work, to tell him what I needed, but he refused to listen. When I wouldn't put out, he started calling me names, and I couldn't deal. I told him he could fucking leave. In fact, he demanded he leave. I called his dad and told him to pick up his loser of a fucking son. I told him if he didn't, I knew where Jet kept the shotgun, and I'd use it if I had to.

I sucked in a deep breath. *Oh my God, Billie. That's a lot of stress. Are you okay?*

Yeah. So, his dad came and parked in the driveway, and Jet tried to get me to sit and talk, and I just lost my shit, told the girls to go to their rooms, and started throwing plates around to get out this anger I feel whenever I see him. I didn't mean to, but I just lost control. I think we only have a couple left. But whatever, he left.

The memory of her throwing a book at his head a couple of weeks ago resurfaced.

Oh damn... that sounds really intense. Are you okay? Are the kids okay?

No. I mean, yes, we are fine. They were pretty worried, but we're fine now. Let's hang out later, and I can explain more. I gotta get breakfast ready now.

I scratched at my head. This was all a bit much. I didn't know how to handle this. It sounded like shit was gunna get ugly, real fast. A shotgun? Really?

Sure. Let me know what you need, babe. I'll see you later. If you need to vent or anything, just call me, okay?

Thanks, Stels. I love you.

Love you too, Billie.

Putting my phone down, I rubbed my face. This was not good. This was really not good. This was beyond what she had said was going on and confirmed my gut that something about their marriage was really, really off. For her to just explode like that... I knew she'd done it before; I'd seen it but in front of her kids?

Hey, babe, one question. You didn't do that because of what happened, right? Like I'm not the reason all this is happening? I fired off the message. I don't know why, but I needed the reassurance.

Her response was immediate. *Lord no. You're my only bright light. Jetland fits the whole description of a goddamn psychopath. He's made me feel small for most of our marriage, and I'm done, Stella. I'm fucking done. He can stay gone for all I give a shit. I deserve better. I know who I am because I no longer have to hide behind being a good little submissive wife. I can be me. Truly me. The girl I lost over time being married to him. He's gotta be blind to treat me like this. I am everything a good wife is, and he still treats me like he can't see me. How can you just ignore your wife? Your kids? How can you listen to the opinions of random women over the opinions of your spouse? It's stupid, and I hate it. Fucking done, bro. Done.*

I breathed a sigh of relief. *Okay, I just wanted to check because I don't want to be responsible for this.*

Not at all, babe, we are good. Don't even worry about it. I love you so much for everything you've done to make me strong.

I put my phone on the kitchen counter. Jesus, this shit is insane. I wanted to talk to Tyler, but he was at work. Thank God it was his last shift before the weekend, and we were going away on a mini vacation this weekend. I was so excited, and I knew he was looking forward to leaving our space and going somewhere else for a couple of days.

I sent him a quick 'good luck at your shift; I love you' text before I went into the garden and began watering my plants. They smelled divine. A mixture of pollinator flowers and fruit trees were in full bloom. Garrett and Max were swimming in the pool.

As much as Billie's shit sucked, I lived a good life, and I had to hold onto that. Sure, Ty and I had our struggles. We were financially in the pits, stress was dragging us down, and we struggled to find time for each other, but we loved what we had created. Even through the loss we've endured, we were happy for the most part. We struggled like everyone else, but I couldn't recall a time he'd ever made me feel the way Jet made Billie feel.

For that, I was grateful.

We'd worked hard to create a life where our kids could be free—playing from morning until evening on a safe street where break-ins and stabbings were unheard of. The city we were attached to was awful for those things, but we were just beyond reach out here. Almost as if when the sun came out, it blessed us with its rays, promising safety and love.

"Mom, mom!" Max yelled from the pool, "Garrett keeps squirting me in the face with his water gun!"

"So? Squirt him back, dude." I rolled my eyes and chuckled. Boys. They were going to be the death of me.

Finally done watering, I grabbed a lawn chair and sprawled out, only to be interrupted by my phone's incessant buzzing. I was almost afraid to pick it up. I didn't want to deal with this shit anymore. I didn't know what to say or how to help. I wasn't in the loop enough to offer any sage advice. My heart clenched as I unlocked the screen, squinting to read the onslaught of screenshots Billie had sent me.

Reading them all, I grew more and more sickened. She was placing the entire blame for their marriage breakdown on him. Which made sense from what she had told me was going on.

But one sentence stuck out in his replies to her, and I couldn't get it out of my head...

Billie, if you don't stop this shit, I am going to leave you. For good this time.

This time... this time...

Had this happened before?

Was it Billie's fault or Jetland's?

The questions swirled in my head as I tried to shake them off. I couldn't help but feel like this was only the beginning of their problems, and I feared, no, dreaded what would come next.

Her texts came in hot and fast.

How fucking dare he act like any of this is my fault. No, I reject that. This is all on him. He treated me like I was expendable; he treated me like shit. I did nothing but be a loving wife. I supported him and his business dreams. I stayed home to tend the kids so he could work and do what he wanted to do. I supported him when he was a start-up, and we had to drain our accounts to buy that first tech company. Through all the women he talked to instead of me, through his stupid lacrosse hobby, I was the one who was there for him. Fuck him, and fuck this. Asshole wants to just come home like nothing happened. No. I am gunna get a lawyer and crush him. I deserve everything he has and what he's put me through.

His soccer. His college. His late nights. His date nights with the boys. Skipping the girl's ballet. Forgetting our anniversary. Everything. I overlooked it all because the bills were paid. Not anymore. Fuck him. I hate him. I've always hated him.

God, I wish he was dead.

I should have listened to my parents and gone to school. I shouldn't have just been a mom. I should have gone to college and become a nurse like I'd planned to. I wouldn't be stuck, then.

I could have been somebody.

God, I never should have left Steve. I'm going to call him tonight. I fucked up, big time. I hope it's not too late, and Steve doesn't have a girlfriend or something. But if he does, I know he will pick me up.

Stella? Why aren't you answering me?

STELLA!!!

"Mom! Mom!" Max yelled again. Irritation flared as I looked up at him, just before getting a face full of water from the water gun.

"Really? Guys! I don't want to get wet! Keep it between you two!" I tried so hard to be a gentle parent, but these boys tested my patience.

Garrett laughed, soaking Max before taunting him. "Nice job, dude; now you made Mom mad."

"I don't care; she is on her phone again! How are we supposed to spend time with you if you are always on your damn phone?" Max yelled at me.

I was shocked at his outburst. "Max! Is that any way to speak to me?"

"Mom, he's right." Garrett suddenly went quiet. "You are always on your phone. You haven't even come in the pool with us all summer."

My heart stopped as I processed his words. *Is this how my children view me?* I broke down and put my phone on the table. "Boys, I am so deeply sorry you feel like I haven't spent time with you. I love you both so much, and I think you're the coolest dudes around. How about I hop in now, and we have splash wars?"

Max's face lit up. "Really?"

"Really, really, you better be ready cuz once I'm back with towels, you're both getting it!" Grabbing my phone, I walked into the house. It was still buzzing as I set it on the counter and turned it on 'Do Not Disturb." A small smile graced my face as I thought how apt that was. All this shit was causing my own family to feel like I wasn't there for them. I'd been so wrapped up in making sure Billie and her kids were safe that I'd forgotten to love on my own.

That changes today.

I grabbed a couple of towels and changed into my bathing suit before exiting the back door, only to be greeted with streams of water hitting me. Instead of getting angry, I gave them my most maniacal grin.

"Oh, you boys are gonna get it!"

And without warning, I launched myself into the pool and dove headfirst into their world of play.

Six

I'm going on a date with Steve.

It would have fallen off if my mouth wasn't attached to my jaw. *Oh?*

Yeah, she texted back; *I figured it's a good time to see what else is out there. Since Jet is gone for good, I need someone else. He's been texting me non-stop. It's quite annoying, and honestly, it sounds really nice to have the distraction. Shark boards and boozy drinks... Who knows what else the night will bring ;)*

I was happy for her, mostly. I wanted her to experience true companionship, but I was also weary. From what I could tell, it felt like she was rebounding, and Steve was mostly nice. Quiet. Kept to himself. He was really only out and about when he was mowing or watering the lawn. But Billie said she knew him from way back, so she must have a better read on him than I did. I think they went to church together.

How could I blame her for wanting to get away from Jet drama? He was suffocating her, and I could see the life being drained out of her every time she spoke about him. She needed this. She needed to feel alive again, and I wouldn't stand in her way of feeling that.

Come around Friday at dinner and help me get ready?

My fingers paused before I typed back a yes with a smiley.

***

Friday night rolled around, and Billie practically vibrated with excitement as she got ready. I hadn't seen her this giddy in a long time. It felt good to see her so happy for once. She'd asked me to come over to help her pick her outfit before she walked to his place. She'd even bought a charcuterie board from one of those fancy places. Really going all out for this date. She put her hair in a high pony with a ribbon; only the end was frayed and slightly shorter than the other. It was kind of endearing.

"You look amazing!" I gushed as she twirled in front of the mirror. The deep red dress clung to her frame, accenting her curves in all the right places, reminding me of how long it had been since I had done something with myself like this. I felt like a potato sack in comparison as I sat on the edge of her bed, playing therapist again.

"Yeah, yeah, I know I should be happy about this, right?" She sat on the chair in front of her dresser. "But what if Jet happens to look at the cams and sees me walking out like this? I'm so nervous about leaving the girls, too. I know they're older, and I have the baby monitor, so I can always watch them and make sure they're okay, but ugh."

"I can always come hang out with them too; Ty is home tonight." I offered, despite not really wanting to. If Jet came home and saw me here and Billie gone, my main concern would be him getting aggressive. And I wanted to spend the night reconnecting with my husband.

"Nah, I got this. I'm just overthinking it. Plus, it's good for them to be alone without me hovering for once. Henley turns 13 next week, so may as well get her used to babysitting now." She breathed deeply, gathering up her purse and keys before hugging me. The scent of her perfume wafted into my nose, a mix of vanilla and cinnamon. "Thank you for everything, Stella, I don't know what I-"

"Hey, hey, no mush now, or you'll have us both tearing up." I playfully wiped my eyes before walking with her to the door. She gave her girls kisses on the way and told them to be good. "You better text me if you need anything. Let me know when you're on your way home. The bears have been hella active around here. You don't want a cougar or something to get a hold of your fine behind!"

We both laughed as she locked the door behind her. We walked past my place, and she continued onto Steve's. The sound of her heels echoed down the dull cement sidewalk as she walked. She turned and gave me a little wave before walking up the front steps and knocking.

I made dinner, got my kids to shower, and tucked them in, checking my phone periodically for a message from her.

Around nine, Tyler popped some popcorn, and we were sitting on the couch, engrossed in some movie about dads doing ridiculous things for their kids. It was hilarious, especially with his random quips accompanying their dialogue as if he was right there alongside them. Glancing at him, I smiled. We'd been working really hard on reconnecting, but he never pressured me for more than what I was able to give at any one moment in time. He allowed me space to exist as I am and peace to grow into who I needed to become.

"Want a foot massage, babe?" He asked, grabbing one of my feet and pressing his thumb into the heel.

I stifled a groan, "Yes, yes, I do."

His hands worked magic on my calloused heels, loosening the tension and allowing me space to forget about the stress of my week.

"So, tell me what's new in the world of Stella, stay-at-home mom extraordinaire."

"Honestly, not much. Just teaching Max some math, and Garrett is flourishing with STEM. It's amazing. Maybe tomorrow we can set up a science experiment and we can show you what we've been doing." I smiled, keeping my eyes closed as he worked my toes.

"I'd love that."

Tilting my head to look at him, I asked, "How are you, Ty? How are things at work? I know it's been really stressful lately. Are things getting any better?"

His expression was pinched and he heaved a sigh, "Sort of. New management has made things a bit more easygoing, but it's still more of the same bullshit. If we weren't trying for a baby, I'd say damn it all to hell and find another job, but if we get pregnant, we will need the extended benefits, and I just can't see anywhere near us offering what my job does."

"Mmmm, yes, right there," I moaned as he pressed into a particularly tense spot right in the center of my foot. "I know, babe. I want you to know that I'm so proud of how hard you work. I know I don't say it enough, but I really am. You're an incredible husband and father; we are so lucky to have you in our lives. Even if we're struggling a bit right now, we are still watering our garden."

"I love you, Mrs. Silver." He dropped my foot and crawled up my body to plant a kiss on my forehead before grabbing the next foot and starting the massage again. "I appreciate the kind words and am proud of you too."

The movie credits rolled, and Tyler yawned, stretching his hands high above his head before grabbing me a blanket. "No chance I can interest you in coming to bed with me?"

Giving him an apologetic smile, I picked up my phone. "I just promised I'd make sure she was okay... the girls are home alone, and I don't want to be held responsible if something happens to them."

"Fair enough, babe. Well, hopefully she messages soon and then you can come be the big spoon."

I stood, crossing the space between us, and gave him a crushing hug, "I love you fiercely. More than yesterday, but not more than I will tomorrow. Have a good sleep, my sweet prince." After whispering good night, I watched him walk down the hall, disappearing into our room, but not before he gave me a little wave. I caught sight of his disappointment and knew staying up would hurt his feelings, but the only reason I was so committed was because I was truly worried about the kids. What if she never makes it home?

As it neared midnight, then one o'clock, then two o'clock, a knot began to form in my stomach. Billie always checked in before she went home when she said she would, sober or not. It was her thing and part of being a mother with an overly protective husband.

My grip tightened on my phone as panic began to set in around three o'clock in the morning. What if Jet had found out? Oh God...

I opened my security camera app and tried to check in to see if there were any notifications of her walking home, but the cams were static. In a panic, I flipped through the days. Nothing for this whole week. Nothing for last week...

The last video was me taking the garbage out two weeks ago.

What the fuck?

"Hey... hey babe." In a slight tizzy, I walked into the bedroom and gently shook Tyler, but he was sleeping like a log. "BABE."

He groaned and rolled over, "What?"

"The cams are down and have been for weeks. What the fuck happened?"

He bolted upright. "That doesn't seem right. I checked them... last week when the delivery driver dropped our food off. What the hell." Rubbing the sleep from his eyes, he rummaged on the nightstand for his phone.

"Hurry up! I'm scared!"

"Stella, honey, calm down. I am sure there is a perfectly reasonable explanation for this." His phone screen lit the room as he searched, his brow creasing into a frown the further back he went.

"See?" I tried to keep my voice quiet so I didn't wake the kids, but there was no denying the high pitch.

He sighed, "I will contact the company tomorrow and see if they can pull something off the cloud. It just... it doesn't make sense."

I shot off a text to Billie, trying to get a response, but it was still radio silent. "Should I go check in on Billie? See if she's home. What if something happened..."

Tyler held me back, "No. Stella. We don't know anything." He was right. I took a deep breath, trying to calm my racing heart. "Let's just call the company first thing in the morning, alright? If we panic, we won't be any good to Billie if something did happen, if we go over there and..." He didn't even want to finish the sentence.

I nodded, but I couldn't shake the feeling that something was very, very wrong with the footprints and now this. It felt targeted, but our neighborhood was so small, so... close-knit. *Who would want to target me?*

"Hey, hey, hey, don't cry babe." Tyler pulled me into his arms. "Everything is okay, I promise."

But deep down, we both knew he couldn't promise that. If this were some targeted thing, obviously, it would be Jet. I'd become close with Billie; maybe he blamed me for her leaving? For gaining her confidence back. But that seemed so dumb. Why wouldn't you be happy if your wife found herself again?

None of this made any sense, but the longer I stewed on it, the more panicked I grew, and panic didn't help anyone.

"Here, I'll make you some of that root tea you drink to soothe your mind, okay?"

This man was so good to me. I didn't deserve him.

"Yeah, yeah, that sounds good. Thanks... for being there. I feel like I'm going crazy." I settled back into the blankets, my phone never far from my side. The kettle clicked on, and then the scrape of the spoon against the mug as he made my tea; I kept refreshing Billie's contact to no avail. Ugh, what the fuck. It was close to four now. If she was still out there with Steve, that was super irresponsible, given her kids were home alone. The knot twisted tighter and tighter until I wanted to puke.

Please, just answer Billie.

Not more than ten minutes later, Ty walked in with a mug of tea, not steaming, because he knew I liked lukewarm drinks. I took it gratefully and almost downed the whole thing like a shot. I needed sleep. This whole thing was eating me alive, and I half wondered if Billie was doing better than me at handling her own shit.

Why was it affecting me so much?

It wasn't long before I was tucked back into bed, and my husband's arm was firmly grasped around my midsection. "Sleep now, baby." He whispered as he kissed my temple. "I've got you."

One last look at my phone, and I sighed. I prayed against all odds that she just forgot to message me and was safe at home with her kids.

My eyelids grew heavy, and they began to close. I vaguely heard the buzz of my phone before it went silent. My arm was too heavy to reach it, and a dreamless void claimed me like a forlorn lover.

Tomorrow...

Seven

The next couple of weeks were more of the same. Play and trauma dumping. She had apologized for not texting me sooner that evening and said she got home around one. I was pretty mad about it but conceded and forgave her all the same. I had been so worried about her, and she didn't even care. Over the next week, she tried to keep it hidden from me that she was seeing Steve, even though I'd been supportive of her. It was puzzling.

We'd never managed to get the footage off the cloud. It was as if those weeks had never happened. I'd found some weird footprints around the garden bed again and a couple of smudged handprints on the wall that led to our bedroom window, but we couldn't figure out if it was just one of the kids turning on the tap or something more sinister. Because the cams were down, we couldn't even check. The tech said it was some kind of hard reset that only someone who understood security systems could do.

Which put Jet on my number one watch list. His company dealt with IT, and he'd mentioned something about being hired as a white hat. Companies employed him to hack into systems and find faults. He would know exactly how to disable ours. But why? I wasn't a threat to his family. If anything, I helped Billie see her sense of worth again. *Did he find that threatening?*

Things had leveled out for the most part, with the new routines being lots of playdates and fun in the sun for the boys. Billie and I would hang out and chat. She even mostly stopped trauma dumping the last week and was focusing on herself and her goals. She wanted to get a job so she didn't need to rely on him to pay child support on time.

I'd pulled back just enough to retain my sanity, focus my time on my husband, and reconnect with my inner child by playing with my kids. It felt like the world had righted, and I was at peace.

Then, out of the blue, everything shifted.

"Jetland has been going to counseling," Billie announced as we walked one morning. We'd been pointing out various weeds that had been growing in the grass when she changed the subject.

"Mmm?"

"Yeah, he's been showing a lot of willingness to change. Which is good because I'm not apologizing, and he needs to put in this work if he wants a chance at reconciliation."

I paused. Just yesterday, she was saying how she was getting a divorce lawyer lined up and how much better she was feeling without him in her life. She'd been happy seeing Steve, so what changed?

"That's great, I guess?" I was honestly at a loss as to what to say. She'd been going on and on for weeks about how horrible he was and how abusive he was, and now she's reconciling? I truly didn't understand this, and it was giving me whiplash.

"I know what you're thinking. But honestly, Stella, he's really trying. He stepped back in his business. He's looking for a buyer for it. He has a lot of interest in the tech innovations he's created and the systems he's designed for web hacking, so there's no real issue if he sells them. We'd be set for life. Without those outside pressures, we have space to work on us."

"You've been doing so well without him, Billie."

"I know..." Her smile was small but hopeful. "I owe it to the kids to at least try and make it work. You know?"

"Yeah... I know." At least Henley and Jennie would see their father more, but at what cost?

An intrusive thought hit me. With Jet selling the business, Billie stood to gain everything by getting back together with him. I'm sure it was worth a rather large sum, and she would be tied up with lawyers for months, if not years, if she divorced him.

Was she trying to fix things because of money? The thought just sat in my stomach and swirled around. I tried to refocus on what she was prattling on about, but I couldn't stop my brain from churning.

"...And honestly, the girls have been doing awful without his guidance. He really is an amazing dad, and I could do worse. It's not like I really have any other options, anyway." She finished with a smile, and my attention snapped back to what she was saying.

Jennie and Henley were the epitome of nightmare children when Jet was home. I'd seen it firsthand over time. I don't know what the hell he did or said to those kids, but they were explosive when he was around. Almost like they were constantly trying to gain his approval, knowing they'd never get it. The fact that she couldn't see it made me feel like I'd never known her at all.

"That's... great." I finally managed, my tone flat and unenthusiastic. Billie seemed to notice as she nudged me playfully with her elbow.

"I know, it's a shock. But, Stella, I really think this time he means it. We... we actually have a date on Friday." She blushed and ducked her face as she said it.

"A date, eh? Fancy." I pasted on a fake smile and swallowed down the bile that was rising in my throat. Why did I feel so betrayed by this? Jetland was her husband, after all. She had every right to make things work. She was one of my good friends, and I wanted her to be happy. I just felt like all this time she'd taken from me, using me to get her through her pain, and not being there for me in any capacity... it hurt. It also just didn't make sense.

"I know, it's crazy, right?" She chortled and continued to prattle on about her plans for the night as we continued our walk. Long gone was the Billie who seemed to be gaining her confidence back. In place of her was a doe-eyed woman who couldn't see the forest for the trees. While she seemed to be lighter in spirit, she also seemed to be smaller, somehow. Defeated. "And then we are going to get iced coffee by the lake. If it goes well, he will move back in next week! Isn't that exciting?"

"I... I guess so?" My heart raced as I thought back on my security cams. I needed to ask. "Hey, babe?"

"Yeah?"

"Do you think Jet has the ability to black out security cams? Like, hack them or something?" I swallowed hard as her face twisted, and she stopped walking. Turning to face me, she studied my expression, which I carefully tried to keep neutral.

"Why would you ask that?" Her voice was small, her eyes wide.

Shit. I've said too much; now she's going to withdraw. "Oh, I was just wondering. I don't know." Fuck, it felt weird to lie to her. To keep this from her.

Clearing her throat, she answered, "I don't really know, Stella. Maybe." She shifted her eyes as she spoke, and something about that movement gave me pause.

She was lying.

"Oh, no reason. I just thought I saw someone in my yard, and when I looked back, I saw that they were gone. Probably just me being paranoid."

"Yeah, probably." She didn't sound convinced, but she also didn't pry further, much to my relief.

I tried to change the subject, "So, Ty is away fishing this weekend, and I'm so excited for him. He needed the break. I think I'm going to make some forts with the boys and swim in the pool. I've been struggling a bit lately with my mental health. Being outside helps."

"I'm sorry to hear that, Stella. I didn't know you were also struggling. I thought it was just me." She offered me a genuine smile before she hugged me close and squeezed me tight. "We should do a girls' day soon, just you, me, and some Pinot Grigio. Decompress and catch up, what do you say?"

"I think that sounds like it's long overdue. We deserve it, Billie." I hugged her back, my heart breaking a little more as I felt the distance between us grow. Something changed today, and I couldn't put my finger on it.

She was silent for a moment before clapping her hands loudly. "Well, I think we're gonna go play in the back. I want to get some lunch ready for the girls. Henley, Jennie!"

"I should probably go, too. Maybe we can come out again later." I watched the kids grab their scooters and bikes and rush towards us.

"That works!" She smiled, her old self shining through for a brief moment before she turned to leave.

As she walked away, I couldn't shake the feeling that the Billie I thought I knew was gone.

Eight

Something's off. Two weeks with hardly any contact. It was like the sun decided to shy away behind a cloud that only hung over Billie's house. Normally, I'd find her out front, messing around in the garden or tossing a ball back and forth with her girls. These days, though, it was like she'd become a ghost in her own life—no eye contact, no chit-chat, just silence and shadows behind closed curtains.

"Hey, Billie," I'd call out when I caught a glimpse of her at the mailbox. But she'd just snatch up her mail and scurry back inside without so much as a nod. I couldn't shake the feeling that something was eating away at her, something more than just the usual stress. I'd seen Jetland with his truck parked there, so I guessed she let him move back in. But it just felt odd that she wasn't texting me or reaching out for the kids to play. It was radio silent.

I whipped out my phone, thumb hovering over her contact name. The screen lit up with our past conversations, all laughter and emojis. Now? It was like pulling teeth. I tapped out a message, trying not to sound as worried as I was.

Morning, Billie! Coffee on me today?

The three dots bubbled up, then disappeared. Minutes dragged by until, finally, the screen blinked with her reply. *Can't. Busy today.*

Everything alright? I texted back, hoping for a crack in the wall she'd built around herself.

Fine. Just busy. Trying to settle back into life with Jet. Short and sweet—that wasn't Billie. Not the Billie I knew, who'd spill her heart out over a cup of lukewarm java.

Alright, if you say so. I responded, but my gut churned with unease. Deep down, I knew 'busy' was code for 'don't ask.' I tossed the phone onto the counter, its clatter echoing my frustration.

I moved through my day, but part of me stayed perched by that phone, waiting for a sign, any sign, that my friend was still there. When night finally fell, and still no word from Billie, the worry gnawed at me like a rat on wires.

"Billie's been... distant," I admitted to my husband over dinner, pushing peas around my plate. "I'm really starting to get worried."

He laid his hand over mine. "Maybe she just needs some time? I know things have been weird since Jet moved back in, but it's another adjustment. Those girls have been through a lot these last few months. The fights, Jet moving out, him moving back in. Maybe they are just trying to figure it out?"

"Maybe," I conceded, though my heart was not in it. Time's one thing, but this felt like something else, something darker. I made a promise to myself right there: I'd help Billie, whatever it took. *She'd do the same for me. Right?* "Has Jet texted or called you or anything?"

"Actually, he did. The day after Billie kicked him out, he sent me a message."

I couldn't hide my shock. "Why didn't you tell me?"

"Because I didn't realize I had to? And because he wanted to tell me his side of things, and I didn't feel right dumping that on you when you already had so much going on."

"What did he say?"

Tyler sighed, "He said that Billie is lying and that she's done this before. She needs help, Stel. I don't know what else to tell you. He essentially said that she will drain you and move on to someone else who will give her the emotional energy she needs to survive."

My lips downturned into something that must have resembled a grimace because Tyler put his hands up, "Woah, babe, this is why I didn't tell you. Don't shoot the messenger."

"I'm sorry. I just... I find that hard to believe. Billie has been nothing but honest with me." But a small voice in the back of my head kept asking, *but was she?*

"Babe, I just don't have a good feeling about this, and I'd prefer you stay out of it entirely. They're weird, and I don't trust them. I don't like how this affects you, and honestly, it would be so much easier if they weren't around."

"How could you SAY that?" I screamed, pushing at his chest, ignoring the way his eyes tightened.

"I'm just trying to protect you! You're making this so much harder than it needs to be, Stella! Just stay away from her!"

I couldn't bear to listen to it anymore, turning on my heel and fleeing to my room.

How could he say that about my best friend?

***

The sun had a way of coaxing life out into the open. Our neighborhood blossomed with life. Kids hopped on bikes, and everyone was out mowing their lawns or tending their gardens. Everyone except the Winters'. Mrs. Callen from two doors down chatted with the mailman, her voice loud, filtering through my half-open window.

"Such a beautiful day, isn't it, Frank?" I heard her say.

"Sure is, Marge! Everything's blooming nicely," Frank replied, his steps upbeat on the sidewalk.

I leaned against the sill, watching, absorbing. But beneath the chatter and cheer, something twitched across the street—a curtain pulled too quickly and the fluttering of movement. I caught myself staring at her front door longer than I should have, waiting for a sign of life. Anything.

"Mom, can we go see if Henley can play?" My son stood beside me, watching the lively neighborhood.

"Uh, not today, honey." I forced a smile. Tyler and I had barely talked the last few days. I hadn't forgiven him for the horrible things he'd said about Billie yet. "Let's give them some space, okay?"

"Okay..." He dragged the word out, loaded with the weight of a thousand whys.

"Go on, scoot. Play with the others." I nudged him gently out the door and toward the yard, Max in tow.

What kind of adjusting they were doing inside that house for them to be so noticeably absent?

***

I paced the living room, my slippers scuffing against the carpet in a back-and-forth rhythm. My thumb moved quickly, scrolling through the last dozen texts to Billie—each one met with vague excuses or hollow promises to catch up soon.

"Tyyyy," I said, drawing out his name in a long exhale. I needed to talk to him about this. We were partners, and I couldn't keep hiding the anxiety I felt. "It's been weeks since she's come out of that house. Weeks."

"Can you just leave it, babe?" He said from the couch, a mild frown furrowing his brow.

"Space is one thing. This is... it's like she's disappearing right before our eyes." I shook my head, the unease settling deep in my bones as I all but ignored him.

"Fine. I'll bite. Just because you're like a dog with a bone, and you won't let it go. Have you tried just going over there?" The suggestion was simple, yet it made sense. If she wouldn't reply to me... maybe if she saw me, she'd open up. To be honest, I was surprised he was suggesting it, given the sour taste our last conversation about Billie had gone.

"Face-to-face, huh?" I mulled over his words. I really didn't want to. After what she said about Jet and their withdrawal, I was worried about what I'd find. "Alright. I'll do it."

"Want me to come with?" Ty's offer hung between us, but I shook my head. That would make things messy.

"Thanks, but no. This is a girl thing. A best friend thing," I said, though I appreciated the gesture.

The walk to her place was short, yet it felt so long. I could feel every heartbeat urging me forward, even as my stomach twisted into knots. Houses with their manicured lawns flanked my path, but my focus tunnel-visioned on one door—her door. Her yard was becoming overgrown with weeds, and her flowers were wilting.

It wasn't too late to turn back, to pretend this was just another Sunday stroll. But no, this was for Billie. My loyalty made it so I needed to see this through.

"Come on, Stella," I muttered to myself. "It's now or never."

My fingers trembled slightly as I reached for the doorbell, its sound echoing ominously behind the closed door. No footsteps followed. My heart pounded a warning, but I raised a hand and knocked anyway.

"Billie, it's me," I called softly, not sure if I was relieved or terrified at the prospect of her not answering. "Can we talk?"

The moments stretched out until, finally, I heard the click of the lock disengaging. The door cracked open, and there she was - my friend, looking like a shadow of herself, but here. Here with me.

"Stella..." Her voice was a whisper, a thread pulling at the silence.

"Hey, Billie." My smile was shaky as I clung to the normalcy of our greeting.

Her gaze didn't rise to meet mine, her eyes shadowed and fixed on something over my shoulder, something distant and untouchable. The door hung ajar between us, like a shield she was reluctant to lower.

"Billie?" I prompted the concern knotting in my chest. "Is everything okay?"

She shifted, a mere silhouette framed by the dimness of her home's interior. "It's fine, Stella. We're just... Jetland's back, right." Her voice caught on his name as if the words were thorns. "We're adjusting."

"Adjusting," I echoed softly, the word hanging heavy with unsaid fears. "I can imagine that's... a lot."

"Yep," she murmured, retreating an inch, the door following her cue.

"Look," I started, the urgency clawing up my throat. "I know things have been tough for you, Billie. I'm worried about you. We all are."

"Stella, I appreciate it, I do, but..." She swallowed hard, her hand hovering near the door handle. "I need to figure this out on my own."

"Figure what out, though?" I pressed, taking a step closer. The space between us felt awkward. Tense. "You don't have to be alone in this. Remember when you sat with me through those endless nights when Tyler got injured at work? You said friends don't keep score, but they do show up."

A flicker of emotion crossed her face, a ghost of our shared connection. Then it was gone, just as quickly as it came.

"Showing up can mean different things," she whispered, almost to herself.

"Then let me be here in whatever way you need," I offered, reaching out a tentative hand, bridging the gap her withdrawal had formed. "Even if it's just to listen or to sit in silence. Whatever it is, babe, you're not alone. You've never been alone."

Her eyes finally met mine, and for a heartbeat, I saw the turmoil churning in their depths, the plea for help she couldn't voice. But then she blinked, and it was veiled once more.

"Thanks," she breathed, her voice so faint it nearly slipped away. "I'll... I'll think about it." She moved to close the door, then stepped forward.

"Jetland... he's changed, you know? Or maybe I have. We're just two strangers trying to remember why we ever fell in love in the first place all those years ago. It's not the same. I don't know who he is anymore... I think... I think I made a mistake." The confession slipped from her lips before she could stop them.

Her hand found mine as she reached across the threshold. "Marriage isn't easy, Billie. It's like a garden; it needs tending, or the weeds take over. But sometimes, you find the soil's gone bad, and no matter how much you water it, nothing will grow."

"Yeah," she sighed. "And I'm just so tired. Tired of pulling weeds and pretending there's still something worth saving."

A tear escaped, tracing a warm path down her cheek. She quickly wiped it away, embarrassed. But I didn't look away or offer empty platitudes.

"Thank you," she whispered. "Sometimes, I think you're the only thing keeping me glued together."

"We all need someone. And right now, I've got enough glue for both of us."

Footsteps sounded at the top of the stairs. Jet's frame came into view as he leaned against the wall. "Billie, the kids are hungry."

She looked panicked before turning away, "Yep, I'll come make food in a minute. Bye Stella."

The click of the door closing in my face sent me into shock. *What the fuck was that?* I lingered on her porch for a second, drawing in a deep breath. Somehow, relief mixed with concern. She'd at least let me in but subsequently shut me out again. The door was closed now, but the issues inside... those remained wide open.

Should I get others involved? I stared at the unruly hedges that lined Billie's property. They were like the boundaries I was afraid to cross between privacy and intervention. Looking back, Jet stood with his arms crossed in their big bay window, his gaze hard. *What the fuck?*

I started walking, my steps slow, deliberate. Each footfall felt like a question—was I doing enough? Was my presence a comfort or just another reminder to Billie of how much she needed to hide?

***

"Stella, you're going to wear a hole in the carpet," my husband called from the kitchen, a playful note in his voice as he got dinner going. I went to join him, washing my hands and then staring outside.

"Sorry," I murmured, not turning away from the window.

He didn't understand, couldn't really. This was about more than just being neighborly—it was about a bond, a commitment to someone who mattered. Billie mattered. Whether or not he believed Jet, I believed Billie, which automatically put us at odds with each other.

I looked across the street. A sudden flicker of movement caught my attention. Jetland's silhouette passed behind the closed curtains of their living room so quickly that I almost missed it. My breath hitched. Was that a raised arm? Oh shit, was that something being thrown? *Goddamn. This shit again.*

"Stella, come on. You can't do anything. Billie made her choice to let him back home. She decided that for her family. Not you, not me, her. It would be best if you let it go," he sighed, but I barely heard him. My eyes were glued to the scene unfolding across the way, my heart pounding in time with the fear that clawed at my insides.

"What the hell is going on in there, Billie?" I whispered.

Just then, the front door of their house creaked open. Billie stepped out onto the porch, her blonde hair wild around her shoulders, the fading light casting long shadows across her face. She wrapped her arms around herself, as if holding the pieces of her together, and looked straight at me—or maybe through me. Her mouth opened slightly as though she was about to call out, to cry for help... But then she shook her head, a tiny, almost imperceptible movement, and retreated inside without a word.

"Dammit," I muttered, fists clenching at my sides. The decision was made for me: I'd have to do something tomorrow, make a call, knock on her door again, or do anything. Because tonight, there was an unmistakable message in the stillness—a heavy, leaden dread that told me the storm was coming. What was happening behind closed doors wasn't good.

I stepped back from the window, and the image of Billie's defeated posture seared into my mind. I thought of her girls and how they deserved a world free of this ever-growing darkness.

"Everything okay?" Tyler asked again, concern threading his words this time as he noticed my blank stare.

"Fine," I said, my voice flat. "It's all fine."

But even as I spoke, my gaze drifted back to the window, to the house across the street where secrets festered and trust eroded. The last of the sun faded, replaced by oppressive darkness.

Tomorrow, I would fight for my friend, for her family. Because what else is friendship for, if not for diving into the fray when the world turns cold?

But by the time tomorrow comes, will I already be too late?

Nine

I glanced down at the phone screen as it buzzed against my hand, my thumb already hovering to swipe the message into view. *We are dead to each other* stared back at me in stark black letters. It was from Billie, and it was like a knife to the chest. My breath hitched as I reread the message for the fourth time.

Stella, for my own sake, for moving on with Jet, I had to tell him about us. You are the reason why I couldn't move on with him. Why I couldn't move past the black cloud. You are the guilt in my heart. The reason I can't sleep, can't eat. I'm sorry, but this means we can't talk again. We are dead to each other.

What? My mind reeled as I sank onto the nearest chair, the phone slipping slightly in my clammy grip. This was a fucking punch to the gut. That kiss was a mistake—a slip in a moment of vulnerability. We said as much, didn't we? My heart pounded against my ribs, echoing the chaos in my thoughts. We'd hung out almost every day since then, and she hadn't spoken a word about it. Was it something else I did?

Was it just me? Was I that awful of a person? I tried so hard to be a good friend; maybe I just... wasn't.

Did I read the months of our friendship afterward wrong? Was she hanging out with me so Henley and Jennie had their friends?

This had to be Jetland's request. It made no sense if it came from her. I got up, my legs somehow supporting the weight of betrayal as I paced the length of the living room. Every step felt heavier than the last. No. I was a good friend. I was a good person. Why would Billie throw her fragile marriage into upheaval over a single kiss yet not reveal her deeper connection with Steve? It didn't make sense. There would be no chance of reconciliation if Jet knew about those dates. He hated Steve. Billie had told me that at one point, she dated Steve, and he had always been her 'one that got away.' So if Jet was still around, she hadn't told him. So, there was only one conclusion...

She wanted to absolve her guilt, over me, over Steve, by only telling Jetland enough to cleanse her soul but not enough to destroy whatever the fuck they were trying to salvage. It was the only reasonable explanation.

And the kids. Oh, my poor boys.

"Think, Stella, think!" I muttered, replaying every conversation, every look exchanged over coffee cups, and every word spoken since. Not once did Billie hint at being anything but okay with how we resolved that night. *Was she just pretending? Or did she really mean this?*

I ran a hand through my hair, gripping the strands tight enough to hurt. The frustration bubbled up inside me, spilling out in uneven breaths. This couldn't be happening. Our families, our kids—they were best friends. And now what? Because of one stupid, thoughtless moment? Everything was over? Just like that? How the fuck do I explain to my kids that they'll never play with their friends again?

"Shit," I cursed under my breath, staring down at the phone in my hand. Billie's name lit up the screen, her words just... there. Mocking me. My finger hovered over the call button, itching to demand answers. But I hesitated. What if Jetland picked up? What if he got angry that I broke this boundary—who knows what he'd do? Maybe Billie truly did hate me. Maybe our friendship had all been a lie.

God, Billie, why? I leaned against the wall, feeling its coolness against my forehead. Betrayal stung, but beneath it all lay a thread of fear—for Billie, for myself, for our kids.

The silence of the house pressed in on me, pulling the breath from my lungs. The kids were in the backyard, and Tyler was fishing. I shot Ty a text, explaining the bare bones before trying to catch my breath. I felt alone, truly alone. I slid down to the floor, knees pulled tight against my chest, and let the phone fall to the carpet with a soft thud. There were no answers here, just echoes of laughter and secrets that now seemed so far away.

***

The late afternoon sun spilled through our kitchen window when I finally called for the kids to come sit at the table. I could hear them abandoning their toys, feet stomping on the floor. They arrived with expectant faces, but my smile was a mask I wasn't sure I could keep in place.

"Hey, guys," I started, the words sticking in my throat, "we need to talk about something." My hands fumbled with the hem of my shirt, avoiding their curious gazes. How do you break a kid's heart, let alone two?

"Is it about Henley and Jennie?" My youngest tilted his head, his eyes wide and unknowing of the hurt that was coming. He'd sensed the shift since Jet moved back home.

I nodded, feeling the weight of every syllable before they even left my mouth. "We... we won't be seeing them for a while." There, I said it. But the look of confusion on their faces made me rush to cushion the blow. "Sometimes, grown-ups go through tough times, and they need a bit of space to figure things out. Auntie Billie and Jet are just... trying to adjust to some stuff."

"But why can't we play together? Did we do something wrong?" The question, so full of innocence, nearly broke me.

"No, no, no, sweetie, you didn't do anything wrong. None of this is your fault, okay? Either of your faults." My voice wavered, betraying the conviction I was trying to project. "It's just something between the adults, and we have to respect that."

They nodded slowly, still not fully grasping the situation. As I gave them each an Xbox controller and set up their screen time, I felt the sting of tears threatening to spill. This wasn't how neighborhoods were supposed to work. You're meant to borrow sugar and watch each other's kids, not... this cold severance. At the very least, the kids should be allowed to see each other, even if it's to say goodbye. After all, how can you just break a heart like that without confronting the fact it was you who did it?

From the living room window, my gaze drifted to the Winters' house across the street. It stood silent, the curtains drawn tight. Billie's once green lawn was now just shades of brown, the flowers dead without her tender care.

How was she handling all of this? Was it her that wanted to end our friendship? Or was it him? The questions swirled in my mind, refusing to give me time to process all this. It didn't make sense. It wouldn't make sense, and I'd never get answers. *Dead to me.*

It was nearly impossible to understand how things had gone from jovial and compassionate to... this.

Why would she bother to tell him after months of telling me everything was fine? After months of us continuing to build our friendship? She hadn't even considered it an issue because she felt he'd been stepping out on her all these years. She said as much. I helped her get ready for a date with another man, for God's sake. My head began to pound as a migraine set in.

Ugh, I needed my husband. My strength. He'd know what to say to calm my nerves. To soothe my frayed edges. Instead, I pulled myself together and got to making dinner so I could settle in and watch a movie with my kids.

I was a mother, after all, and nothing outside of these four walls mattered more than ensuring my children were safe.

Physically and mentally.

***

It was hardly six a.m. when I stepped onto my porch, a steaming mug of coffee my only companion. That's when I saw it—a splash of red and white that seemed alien against the brown and green of their tree hedges. A "For Sale" sign, bold and unapologetic, stood where yesterday there had been nothing but overgrown grass, now neatly cut and weeded.

My breath hitched, and the mug trembled in my hand, sloshing hot liquid over the rim. Wow. This was extreme.

"Must be some mistake," I murmured, hoping the words might make it disappear.

They didn't.

Cars started pulling up before I had the chance to process the sign's presence—curious eyes peering out from behind rolled-down windows, measuring, evaluating. Strangers tread on the paths where my children played. This must have been planned. There's no way they did this overnight. How the hell does moving solve any of their problems?

"Mommy, who are those people?" My youngest whined while rubbing sleep out of his eyes.

"Nobody, honey," I replied, though the lie tasted bitter on my tongue. "Just... lost travelers, I guess."

I retreated inside, ushering my kids in first and shutting the door, leaving the spectacle of the sign and its parade of viewers behind. Our neighborhood was highly sought after, with a low move-out rate, and this opened the floodgates for us to become like animals in a zoo.

The weight of Billie's last message pressed down on me as I paced the kitchen. Back and forth, back and forth—a caged animal in my own home. I couldn't stop ruminating over it. We were more than neighbors; we were confidants and allies in the chaos of suburban motherhood. Best friends. Or so I thought. I must have been wildly wrong about what our friendship meant to her if she so easily threw it away.

Confront her. Get answers, part of me insisted, rage bubbling inside me. Not just for me. For my kids. For the loss they felt. The tears they shed as I'd tucked them into bed the night before.

But no—in my non-response to her message, I'd promised space, hadn't I? Promised to respect whatever boundaries she needed to mend what had broken between her and Jet. Wasn't that what friends did? Stand in the gap when storms threatened to wash everything away? If that were true, why did I feel like she was the storm and she had drowned me and spit me on the shore like nothing more than trash unearthed from the bottom of the sea?

Tyler's words came back to haunt me. *She will drain you and move on to someone else who can feed her emotional energy.*

"Disposable," I whispered, the word tasting like ash. *Was that all our time together amounted to?* A convenience easily discarded when the road got rough. I understood wanting to come clean. But if she'd wanted a clean slate with him, why was she hiding a far bigger issue than that kiss? Nothing made sense anymore, but one thing rang true: my husband had been right. I should have left well enough alone and stood up for myself weeks ago. Way before I became so entrenched in her life that it felt like I was a part of it.

The sign outside taunted me, a harbinger of changes yet to come and friendships too fractured to mend. And all I could do was watch, wait, and wonder if the life I knew was slipping through my fingers.

Ten

I swiped the screen of my phone for what must have been the hundredth time today, double-checking that my phone wasn't on silent. No messages. Billie's absence was a gaping void, filled only with the phantom buzzes I imagined every few minutes.

"Any word?" Tyler's voice drifts in from the doorway, gentle as he could be. He knew the answer before I shook my head, the motion more of a shudder. He'd been back for a couple of days, and after I told him what had happened, he was shocked. He had held me as I cried and thought I didn't notice when he pounded out an angry text to Jet over hurting his wife. I loved that he was my protector. Always.

He crossed the room. When he wrapped his arms around me, it was calming. Solid. Safe. Come hell or high water, this man stood by me from the first day we laid eyes on each other, and he continued to do so, even as he held me together with the strength of his touch.

"We did everything we could, Stella," he said, resting his chin atop my head. His chest rumbled, and for a moment, I wanted to believe him. "We've been there for her through everything. You the most. You were a good friend, babe. You didn't do anything wrong."

I nodded against him, but my heart wasn't in it. "Maybe she was scared," I ventured, my voice barely above a whisper. "You know how controlling Jet can be. Maybe she thought—"

"Thought what?" Tyler prompted when I trailed off, lost in the maze of 'what ifs.'

"Maybe she thought it was the only way out. To push everyone away." The words tasted bitter, laced with the sting of abandonment. "But why like this? Why now? She had months to come clean. She could have said something all that time, but she was adamant that she hated him. Maybe this whole time, she just hated me."

Tyler sighed a heavy, weary sound. "I don't know, love. I wish I did." He pulled back just enough to look at me, his green eyes searching mine for answers neither of us had. "But you can't force her to talk to you. We can't fix what we don't understand. I'm sad for the boys, but maybe if they leave, a new family will move in, and they will make new friends. Perhaps it's all for the best anyhow." It amazed me how he didn't lord over my head the text Jet had sent, telling me that it was coming and it shouldn't be such a surprise. Not many people could hold in the 'I told you so's,' and yet he didn't mention it. He just allowed me space to process my grief.

I bit my lip, the frustration simmering beneath the surface—the need to do something, anything, gnawed at me. I wanted answers.

"Maybe she'll come around," Tyler added, kissing my head before letting me go.

"Maybe," I echoed, but the word felt like a lie on my tongue.

We were grasping at straws, trying to piece together a puzzle with half the missing pieces. "Come, let's go to bed. The boys have been asleep for hours, and we have the block party tomorrow. Maybe they will come."

Sighing, I let him lead me to the bedroom and shut the door behind him.

***

I slid the last folding chair into place, the metal legs scraping against my driveway with a finality that made me wince. It wasn't the grand community gathering I had once envisioned with Billie by my side, but it was something—a smattering of neighbors clutching paper cups and chitchatting beneath the string lights I had hung up hours before.

"Looks great, Stella," offered Janet from down the street, her smile genuine but her eyes skimming the space for someone else. Someone who wasn't there. "Thanks," I replied, my voice threading through the murmurs of the small crowd. "It's nothing fancy, just... you know, trying to keep things lively."

But the word 'lively' felt like a lie because every laugh felt stifled, and each conversation seemed to circle back to the absence, the only family who hadn't come.

My children darted among adults, their giggles piercing the evening air as they chased fireflies that flickered like distant stars fallen to earth. I watched them, envious of their easy joy, and forced my feet to move, to mingle.

"Hey, did you hear the Winters' are moving?" whispered Sarah, sidling up to me with a conspiratorial glance.

"I did. The sign is literally right there." Her smile faltered, and I realized I'd been snippy.

"Stella, you okay?" Sarah's hand was light on my arm, pulling me back.

"Yeah, sorry. Just really hot," I said too quickly, plastering on a smile that crumpled at the edges. "Just got lost in thought for a second."

She nodded, understanding or pretending to do so, and we lapsed into silence. We weren't friends, so neither of us felt the need to press any further.

"Let's get another round of drinks going!" I called out more to break the quiet than anything else. The neighbors rallied, grateful for the cool beer on such a hot day, and I lost myself in the motions of pouring and serving, laughing on cue. Eventually, the novelty of our gathering wore off, and everyone wandered home.

"Stella," Tyler said after we'd cleaned and the kids were tucked in bed, "you did well tonight."

"Did I?"

"Yeah, you did." He pulled me close. "You're doing the best you can."

And maybe he was right. Maybe this was the best anyone could do—forge ahead and build new bridges even as we carried remnants of old ones within us. "Thanks, babe, I'm trying."

It didn't take long before we drifted off to sleep, the low murmur of some reality TV show the only noise in the house.

The clatter outside yanked me from sleep, a harsh sound that shattered the stillness of the night. I stumbled from our bed, my heart thudding wildly. In the dim glow of the moonlight, I peered out the window, squinting into the darkness.

"Tyler," I whispered, nudging him awake. "Something's happening in the yard."

He grunted, a muffled noise of protest, but I was already pulling on my robe and tiptoeing across the cold floorboards. A thump, and

I knew he was not far behind me. The front door creaked as I eased it open, flicking on the lights as I went.

Once a tidy array of colors and scents, my garden was a chaos of broken stems and scattered dirt. My favorite flowerpots, the ones with the delicate painted lilies, lay in fragments, their beauty lost amidst the wreckage. Anger flared hot and sudden, but an icy dread quickly doused it.

The sound of feet against gravel was startling and my eyes squinted as I tried to make out who was out there. "Hey!!!" I shouted, "STOP!" But the figure booked it until I couldn't see past the darkness that shrouded our yard.

"Who would do this?" I murmured to myself, kneeling to pick up a shard of ceramic. Tyler and I had painted these at the ceramics shop in town. It was sharp, and it sliced my finger open. Quickly shoving my finger in my mouth, I gasped.

The mess didn't end there. Garbage bags had been torn open, their contents strewn across the lawn in a grotesque display. I felt bile rise in my throat as I recognized scraps of our life—drawings from the kids, old bills, remnants of meals.

"Stella, come back inside," Tyler said, grabbing my hand, his voice tinged with concern. "It's not safe. We can look at the cams and see who it was. Please, babe. Stop."

I nodded, but a pitiful clucking reached my ears as I turned to head back. The chicken coop, carefully secured from predators, had been opened. Feathers littered the ground, leading off into the shadows where our chickens had fled, driven by instinct or fear. They'd find their way back, I was sure of it, but it didn't make the feeling of being violated any less real.

"Damn it," I swore under my breath. My fingers curled into fists, nails digging crescents into my palms. This wasn't just random vandalism; it was targeted, personal. And it scared me more than I wanted to admit. Fucking hell.

Back inside, the warmth of the house hit me, but it couldn't chase away the cold knot of anxiety in my gut. As Tyler locked the door behind us, I leaned against the wall, the weight of everything pressing in. He opened his security cam app and started searching for footage, but the person responsible had kept their face carefully out of view. The only real image we got was a black hoody, and a baseball cap pulled low.

"Billie," I said softly, the name slipping out before I could stop it. Would she do this? The thought was absurd, offensive even, but it lodged itself in my mind. She was hurting, yes, but surely not capable of—

"Let's call the police," Tyler suggested, his hand resting gently on my shoulder. "They can handle this."

"Right," I agreed, though part of me recoiled at involving anyone else. This was our problem, mine and Billie's, whatever twisted form it took. But I dialed anyway, the numbers a familiar dance under my fingertips.

As I spoke with the dispatcher, my gaze wandered to the dark silhouette of the Winters' house. Would she actually do this? I guess she would if she hated me enough.

"Thank you," I told the officer on the phone, my voice steady despite the tremors inside. "Appreciate your time." Looking at my husband, I sighed and hung up. "They said there's no officers available, and unless it was life or death, they won't be coming out. Just file a report online and let it go, basically."

I moved to the living room, sinking into the couch as exhaustion tugged at my eyelids. Thank God the kids were heavy sleepers. This would have terrified them. Tyler sat beside me, his presence a silent support. I rested my head against his shoulder, closing my eyes, but sleep was a distant dream. Instead, images flickered behind my lids—broken pots, scattered trash, empty coop. This was anger. But not rage. Not yet.

"Get some sleep. You're safe. I've got you." Tyler murmured, his breath warm against my hair. "I'll stay up in case they come back."

"Night," I murmured, my eyelids too heavy to fight any longer.

We had to put a stop to this before anything more violent happened.

Suddenly, a memory surfaced—the piece of mirror from the field that day. I'd never searched back in the records to see what, if anything, we could see about what happened there.

Maybe it would have the answer—the key to what the hell was happening.

Tomorrow... I'll look tomorrow...

Eleven

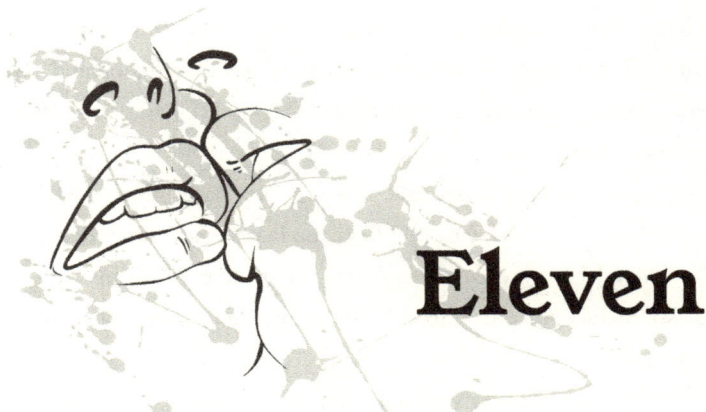

I had leaned against the worn fence, arms crossed, feeling the morning chill nipping at my cheeks. The neighborhood had transformed into a scene reminiscent of those post-apocalyptic movies where everyone simply vanished. No kids raced their bikes down the sidewalk; no savory scents wafted from weekend barbecues – just an eerie silence that pressed down relentlessly. Across the street, their house stood like a black-and-white photograph, devoid of color and life. Their truck was gone, and the little white sedan was parked neatly in front of the house. It had been missing for almost two weeks now, with no sign of them coming in or out.

The once meticulously trimmed lawn is now surrendered to encroaching weeds, and rebellious greenery is reclaiming the territory. No more care about keeping things looking fresh for prospective buyers; the sign is dangling haphazardly. Billie's beloved sun-yellow curtains were drawn shut tight, concealing whatever lay behind them. Not a single movement stirred behind the glass panes. What was happening inside? Where were they? Did they buy a house already without selling this one first and just move without a trace? If they'd been gone this whole time, then it couldn't have been her that trashed our yard. Maybe just some dumb kids.

"Dammit," I muttered in frustration as a wave of emotions surged within me. "This isn't right." I could almost hear Garrett's gentle voice and see Henley's boundless energy that used to light up the block – both were absent now, as if life had been paused without anyone hitting play again.

"Where are you, Billie?" I questioned the silent abode, half-expecting a response that never came. Only my breath fogged up in the crisp air and the distant hum of a world moving forward without them.

A black sedan later pulled up to the curb; some guy emerged in his formal suit that clashed with our suburban setting. His sharp eyes scanned over the neglected Winters' residence with an air of expectation as he knocked on their door fruitlessly before being ushered inside by the realtor.

As they disappeared inside with finality echoing through each closing door click, I wished futilely for the Winters' return—some sign of life.

Steve approached casually, his hands stuffed in the pockets of his faded jeans. "Stella," he started nodding towards the vacant house, "Have you noticed anything... off around here recently?"

I shook my head, my hair brushing against my cheeks—a familiar motion that offered no comfort this time. "Yeah. It's like they vanished into thin air."

"Strange," he mused, scratching the back of his neck in the way he did when something puzzled him. His eyes were squinted, not from the sun but from concern. "You'd think someone would've seen something, you know? We were... we were getting somewhere, and then out of nowhere, she ghosts me."

"Yeah," I murmured, feeling that same knot of anxiety tightening in my stomach.

His hands turned into fists, curling and uncurling as he looked at their place. "It just doesn't make sense. I hate being ghosted, and she isn't reachable by text or social media. What the fuck did I do to deserve this? I knew I shouldn't have let her back into my life. My brother said she'd destroy me again, and it looks like he was right."

I put a comforting hand on his shoulder. "I'm so sorry, Steve. I feel the same way you do. Ghosted."

He grimaced, his face twisting into a scowl. "She'll get what's coming to her. Karma, or whatever else is out there. Deserves it, the way she treats people. Using them and discarding them like trash."

Our exchange was cut short by the sound of hushed voices drifting from the sidewalk where a cluster of neighbors had gathered. I could tell from their furtive glances and the way they leaned in close that they were trying to see who was viewing the property. Gossip was spreading as their absence grew.

"Maybe they won the lottery and skipped town," Mrs. Peterson suggested, her voice tinged with a hope that sounded more like jealousy.

"Or maybe it's something darker," someone countered, his brow furrowed, casting a shadow over his face that matched the ominous tone of his words.

"Could be a family emergency," another neighbor chimed in, trying to inject a reasonable explanation into the mix.

"Family emergency?" Steve scoffed lightly, though there was no humor in his voice. "For weeks on end, with no word to anyone?"

"Doesn't add up," I said, finally stepping closer to join the group. "Billie is—was—my friend," I admitted, though the past tense slipped out unintentionally, making my heart skip a beat. "She wouldn't just leave without saying goodbye. Not unless..."

"Unless what?" Mrs. Peterson prompted, leaning in.

"Unless she couldn't," I finished the weight of what I was implying settling over us. Silence fell again, only now it felt heavy, charged with the fear of unknowns and the gravity of our theories.

"Has anyone tried reaching out?" I asked, hoping someone might dispel the dread creeping up my spine.

There were shakes of heads and shrugs of shoulders, but no one had any concrete answers. We were all grasping at straws, trying to weave them into something that made sense.

"Something's not right," I said, more to myself than anyone else. "It just isn't."

A few minutes later, the door to their house swung open, creaking on its hinges like it hadn't been used in ages. The realtor stepped out onto the porch; a clipboard clutched in her hands that seemed to hold all the answers in the world—or none at all. With a heavy exhale that carried all the way across the lawn to where I stood, she let out a sigh that seemed to deflate her. The man hurried to his vehicle and sped down the street, past the nosy neighbors as I watched through squinted eyes.

"Any luck?" I called out, crossing the street with quick, uneven steps. My voice was louder than I'd intended, echoing off the quiet houses around us.

She turned towards me, her eyes wide with a kind of startled confusion, as if she'd forgotten anyone else existed on this street. "Oh," she said, looking me up and down. "Are you...?"

"Stella Silver from over there. Not a buyer," I clarified, gesturing towards the empty house behind her with a nod. "Just concerned about Billie and her family. Have you heard anything from them?"

Her lips pressed together in a thin line, and she shook her head slowly. "No, nothing. It's been weeks. I've been trying to call, to reach out about a potential sale," she admitted, tapping her fingers against the clipboard. "But every time I call, it just rings and rings."

"Strange, right?" Despite the warm afternoon sun, I couldn't keep the tremor out of my voice or the shiver that ran through me. "They wouldn't just disappear without telling someone. Without telling me." That might have been true... before.

"Right," she echoed, her gaze dropping to her sensible flats. "It doesn't make any sense."

I nodded, though my mind was racing with darker thoughts. *Billie, where are you?*

"Thanks," I murmured, already turning back towards the knot of neighbors still gathered on the sidewalk. The realtor's presence had been a brief interlude but offered no solace, only deepening the pit in my stomach.

"Of course. It's dumb. I want to sell this house; they seemed to be in a real rush to get out of here; now it's costing them the sale they needed," she half-yelled, but I barely heard her over the sound of my footsteps hurrying away. Something had to be done. We needed answers, and soon.

The unease was a living thing, writhing in my gut as I rejoined the cluster of neighbors. Their low murmur of conversation sounded alien. I was mulling over what the realtor had said about them being unreachable. Wherever my gaze landed—on the frazzled mother juggling her toddler on her hip or the old man with his hands buried deep in his cardigan pockets—I found only mirrors of my confusion.

"Stella, you okay?" Steve's voice cut through the fog of my thoughts, his brows knitted with concern.

"Fine," I lied, forcing a smile that felt like plaster cracking on an old wall. We were all pretending, weren't we? Pretending that the quiet was normal, the Winters' house wasn't screaming its emptiness at us from across the street. I looked at their home again. It was just all so... weird. An overreaction that turned into something so big that it left us all confused, reeling from their sudden departure from our lives.

"Maybe we should start knocking on doors, see if anyone knows something we don't. Maybe we can canvass other neighborhoods? We've all kind of exhausted the houses here, and none of us know anything, but maybe the next street over does." The words spilled out before I could stop them, and I clutched at the idea like a life raft. "Someone has to know something."

"Who cares? She wants to disappear; let her. She's hurt enough people in her wake." Steve scowled before turning on his heel and stomping off.

"Could be nothing. Maybe they just went camping," someone else chimed in, but the hollow note in their assurance rang false. It could be nothing, yet here we stood, gathered like mourners at a vigil for a family that had vanished into thin air.

I was about to suggest we split up and canvas the neighborhood when the silence shattered—the discordant wail of a siren sliced through the stillness. Heads turned as one, every pair of eyes locking onto the black-and-white cruiser rolling down our street.

"Police..." The word was a whisper in the air, tinged with a mixture of relief and fresh anxiety. Was this it? Were they here to tell us what had happened to Billie and her girls?

The cruiser slowed to a crawl, passing by their house without stopping, the officer inside taking in the scene with inscrutable eyes. As the car continued on, the taut string of tension among us frayed and snapped.

"Are they looking for someone?" The question came from Mrs. Henderson, her hand fluttering to her throat.

"Or something."

"Maybe they know what happened to Billie," I said, more to myself than anyone else. There was a quiver in my voice that I couldn't control—a tremor of fear, of loyalty to a friend who had become like family. One who had discarded me like I meant nothing.

We watched the police car disappear around the bend, and in its wake, a renewed flurry of speculation took flight. Accusations, theories, wild guesses... they buzzed around me. I couldn't escape. I needed to escape.

Billie wouldn't just leave, not without a word, not without a sign.

And I wouldn't rest until I found out why. It's not like she would care, but I needed to know because even though she tossed me, I still cared about her. I cared that she was safe and unharmed. I cared about her girls deeply, having watched them grow for the last decade.

I still cared.

I made my way around the bend to the curb as the cruiser crept back into view. The officer inside seemed to scan every detail of our neighborhood as he typed on his laptop.

"Excuse me, Officer?" I rapped on his window so I didn't startle him. He looked up, an eyebrow raised in silent invitation for me to continue. "I was just wondering... is there any news about the Winters family? That's why you're here, isn't it?"

He considered me for a moment, his eyes a shade of blue you don't forget—sharp, like shards of ice. "We're conducting an investigation; it has nothing to do with them," he said curtly, revealing nothing more but the hint of caution in his tone.

"Have there been any reports about their family?" I pressed, hoping for something tangible to grasp onto—a crumb, a clue, anything.

"No." With that, the window rolled up, severing our connection and leaving me stranded with more questions than answers.

Turning back to my house, I took in the familiar facade, the windows reflecting the afternoon sun, my own reflection staring back at me—a woman on edge, her calm demeanor a thin veil over the tempest brewing within. My kids played in the back with Tyler, who knew I was worried and gave me space to figure out what I needed.

Once inside, I sank into the silence, the weight of worry settling heavily on my shoulders. The walls around me felt too close, the air too still. I grabbed my phone, thumb hovering over Billie's contact. I wanted to respect her wishes, but this... this was different.

Billie, I'm worried about you, I typed, my thumbs moving with purposeful haste. *I know boundaries, but... please tell me nothing's happened. Anything. We're all worried about you and the kids.*

I hit send, watching the message float into the digital void, waiting for those three little dots to appear, signaling a response that would chase away the fear clawing at my insides.

But there was nothing. There is no typing indicator and no immediate reply. Just the silent echo of my own concern bouncing off a screen that offered no comfort.

The phone lay heavy in my hand, a modern-day Pandora's box filled with both connection and isolation. And as the light faded outside, and neighbors quit gossiping and went home, I fought back tears.

What if Jetland did something to her?

Something that couldn't be undone?

"Stella, you're killing yourself with this. Move on. Please, babe. I am begging you." Tyler's concern strained behind his eyes as his wet body leaned against the doorframe. "You... you've lost weight, you aren't eating, you're just so caught up in this. Let the Winters do what they need to do and move on. Please. They don't matter anymore."

With a sigh, my legs carried me to him, his arms opening to crush me in a hug. "Okay babe... okay..."

He was right. I was making a mountain out of a molehill. They'd probably just moved before selling; it happened all the time. Not everything was sinister and twisted.

"Good girl. Now come swim; the boys and I are waiting."

Twelve

The sun had a certain kind of arrogance that morning, barging through the blinds with no regard for my desire to linger in bed. I stretched, toe to crown, feeling the remnants of sleep peel away from me. A month had flitted past since the whole Billie episode, and like last night's dreams, it had begun to fade into something indistinct—a shadow just out of reach. The neighborhood had all but gone back to normal. I'd just... accepted that they were never coming back. The creepy shit had stopped. Probably just some dumb teenager. Or a bear.

We never got the cameras fixed enough to see what had happened that night, and they went down. Whoever it was in the cap had never been identified either because the cops never cared enough to take a statement. So, I let it go.

"Mom?" My youngest, Max, called from down the hall, his voice the embodiment of boyish impatience.

"Coming!" I hollered back, smiling. Ever since he called me out about being on my phone too much, I'd made an effort to truly be present, which made all the difference. He was a completely different kid. Happier. And so was I.

As I descended the staircase, sunlight washed over me, a warm embrace promising new beginnings. I'd made peace with Billie's silence. Some friendships, it seemed, were just meant to be chapters, not entire books. With each step, the excitement of the day grew stronger.

"Look, Mom!" Garrett shouted, pointing out the window at the flurry of activity across the street.

"Quite the spectacle," I agreed, peering out to see the landscapers pulling up. Their trucks were an organized mess of rakes, shovels, and the promise of manicured beauty. It was as if the Winters' house had been holding its breath all this time, and now it could finally exhale.

"Did the Winters get a gardening obsession overnight or something?" Max pressed his nose against the glass, leaving a smudge that would annoy me later but seemed trivial now.

"Or maybe they're fixing it cuz they sold," Garrett chimed in, noticing the one guy taking down the for-sale sign. "I wish they didn't. I'm gonna miss Henley."

"Could be." I watched the landscapers unload. They moved with purpose.

"Let's watch them for a bit," Garrett suggested, his eyes already lit with the spark of curiosity that so defined him.

"Sure." I smiled. "But let's keep a respectful distance. You know how you're both tornadoes around delicate things."

"Hey, we're not that bad," Max protested, but the grin on his face told a different story—one of toppled vases and crayon masterpieces on hallway walls.

"Come on; I'll make some tea and get you, boys, some juice. We can sit on the porch and take it all in." I ushered them towards the kitchen, their chatter a comforting melody rising above the hum of distant lawnmowers. Tyler came up behind me and held me, breathing in my shampoo as he looked out the window at the spectacle across the street.

"You okay?"

"Mhmm. I've let it go. No longer my issue."

He kissed my neck. "Good. You deserve better, babe. You're amazing." He grabbed Garrett and tousled his hair, "Come, let's go watch while mom makes her tea."

I followed after my bag had steeped, the soft grass cool beneath my bare feet, my eyes squinting against the bright light. There was something deeply satisfying about watching these landscapers shape the world to their will, defining borders and coaxing life from the soil. It spoke of new beginnings, of moving forward.

"Morning," I greeted them with a nod, standing back to admire their handiwork. It was just another day, another shift in the grand scheme of things, but somehow, it felt significant—the closing of one door and the opening of another.

"Whoa, look at that one!" Garrett's voice pierced the calm, his finger pointing towards a particularly vibrant patch where marigolds had been freshly planted. "Can we plant something, too, Mom?"

Not to be outdone, Max bounced on the balls of his feet, his eyes wide with the wonder that only children could hold. "Yeah, can we? Please?" His eagerness was catching

"Sure," I smiled, the thought of dirt under my nails and sun on our backs appealing. Surely, the landscapers wouldn't mind a couple of little helpers. It's not like their yard belonged to some millionaires or anything. "Let's ask if there's something we can do."

The boys wasted no time, scampering over to the gardeners with me trailing behind. It wasn't long before they were handed small watering cans, the water sloshing over the sides as they tottered toward the newly planted flowers. Watching them, this surge of love welled up in me, fierce and protective—my two boys, trying so hard to be gentle with the fragile blooms.

"Careful now," I cautioned, my voice soft but firm. "Treat them like you would a little puppy, gently."

Garrett nodded solemnly, his tongue peeking out from the corner of his mouth as he focused on the task. Meanwhile, Max giggled as a butterfly fluttered past, his watering a bit more haphazard but joyful.

"Mom, it's like we're giving them a little shower!" Max exclaimed, his laughter mingling with the sound of trickling water.

"Exactly," I agreed, watching them with a contentment that filled me to the brim. This, right here, was what mattered—these moments of shared discovery, the simple joy of nurturing life. Not everything that had come before. Not Billie's bullshit.

"Bet I can water more than you," Garrett challenged, his competitive streak flaring as he eyed his younger brother.

"Bet you can't!" Max shot back, concentrating on going faster.

"Boys, remember, it's not about how much, but how well," I reminded them, though I couldn't help the grin tugging at my lips. "Each flower needs just enough to drink."

"Got it, Mom," they chorused, and I stepped back to let them work, my heart full, my worries for once taking a backseat to the simple pleasure of a sunny day spent with family.

I edged closer to the landscapers, my gaze lingering on the neat lines they carved into the earth. The hum of their tools was a gentle buzz in my ears, oddly soothing against the backdrop of my boys' excited chatter.

"Hey there," I called out, catching the attention of a young man with soil-darkened hands. "You're doing a wonderful job."

He wiped his brow with the back of his hand and smiled with a hint of pride. "Thank you, ma'am. We aim to please."

"Stella," I said. My eyes shifted to where the Winters' house loomed. "You wouldn't happen to know where they went, would you?" I know Tyler would be pissed if he knew I asked, but I couldn't help myself. Curiosity killed the cat or something.

The landscaper leaned on his spade, considering my question. "Been dealing with the realtor's assistant or something, said the family is away camping or visiting family, dunno really. The realtor said the place sold and needed a makeover."

"Thanks for letting me know." Relief flooded me. I guess they'd just been visiting family and camping this whole time. Maybe they'd done an across-state trip or something.

"Anytime, Stella." He tipped an imaginary hat, then returned to his work, muscles moving with practiced ease.

I turned back to my boys, that dull ache settling into my chest, the joy of flowers fading into the background. "Come, let's find my seeds and plant some in our yard. We've overstayed."

"But mom!"

"No buts, Max... let's go."

With downcast faces, they handed the landscapers back their watering cans, and we headed back home. I rummaged and found some old seeds, and we set to work, planting them in our garden beds, which was the task that took up most of the day.

The sun arced higher, casting a golden sheen over the day as we lingered outside. That's when they arrived: movers with their truck, its sides emblazoned with "New Horizons" in looping script. They backed into the Winters' driveway, narrowly avoiding the landscaping truck.

"Look at that, Mom," Max commented, his young voice full of curiosity rather than sadness.

I watched as they hauled out an overstuffed armchair; the fabric faded from years of sunlight streaming through windows. Damn, this was happening so quickly. Boxes followed suit, stacked with precision in the back of the truck. Billie's dining table, where we'd shared countless coffees and confessions, was maneuvered carefully down the steps, the movers' gloves obscuring the scratches and stains of family dinners and homework sessions.

"Remember when we helped them pick out that couch?" Garrett asked, nudging me gently.

"Couldn't forget if I tried," I replied, the memory bittersweet on my tongue. Billie had brought all of us because she needed to make sure the couch could withstand four active children before buying it. We'd planned for a whole life together. I bit back the memory.

Tyler came up behind me, his strong arms enveloping me in a familiar embrace. The scent of his aftershave mingled with the soil on my shirt, rooting me back to here and now.

"Stel," he murmured, his voice a low rumble against my ear, "it's just moving vans and boxes. The neighborhood gossip and the worry over Billie were nothing. They've very clearly moved on. You promised me you did, too. This friendship... it wasn't meant for life. You'll find one that is. I promise. You gotta let them go."

My eyes lingered on the house, the stark emptiness of the windows where curtains once danced. I could almost see Billie there, waving goodbye, her smile tinged with the sorrow of unsaid words.

"Let's not lose sleep over shadows and what-ifs," Tyler continued, his thumb drawing small circles on my shoulder. "We've got our own lives to live, our own stories to write. I'm your bestie." He drawled the last word, trying to get me to giggle.

"Yeah," I breathed, allowing his certainty to seep into the cracks of my doubt. "Yeah, you're right."

"Come on," he said gently, guiding me back toward our home, our reality. "Let's go check on those boys of ours, huh?"

"Okay." I allowed one last glance at the truck, its belly now full of the remnants of a life in transition, before turning away. The chapter was closing, and the pages of Billie's story in this neighborhood turned for the final time.

***

The scent of fresh garlic and rosemary wafted through the kitchen as we began making dinner. "Let's make something special," I suggested, pulling out pots and pans more enthusiastically than I'd felt in weeks.

"Garlic knots!" Max exclaimed, his eyes alight with the thought of buttery, carb-filled bliss.

"And spaghetti!" Garrett added, nearly toppling over a stool in his rush to grab the pasta box from the pantry.

"Spaghetti it is," I smiled, watching them scurry around like little chefs on a mission. We fell into an easy rhythm, chopping, stirring, laughing over splattered sauce—our kitchen transforming into a haven where the sizzle of onions in hot oil banished fears.

Tyler's steady hands guided mine as we twirled dough into knots. "You're getting the hang of it," he said, and I couldn't help but lean into his touch. He was a master at this, and I loved the feel of his body on mine.

"Mom, you're squishing them too hard!" Max pointed out, giggling at my less-than-perfect attempts.

"Hey, they're rustic; that's the style now," I defended with a playful nudge, earning another round of laughter.

As the sun dipped below the horizon, we carried plates piled high with spaghetti into the dining room. The conversation flowed effortlessly, stories from school and work filling the house with laughter and love.

"Who's ready for movie night?" Tyler announced as he cleared the last of the dishes.

"Me!" the boys chorused, racing to the living room and diving onto the couch, their earlier energy not even slightly dimmed by the hearty meal.

"Okay, okay, let me see what we've got here…" I rummaged through our collection of DVDs, the familiar titles a comfort in themselves. Finally, I held up a classic comedy, the kind that promised mindless laughs and easy entertainment.

"Perfect choice, babe," Tyler grinned, dimples deepening as he settled beside me on the couch, an arm snaking around my shoulders.

Wrapped in a cocoon of blankets and family, I sank deeper into the cushions, allowing the flickering images on the screen to chase away the remnants of sadness. The room echoed with our combined chuckles.

"Remember when we used to quote this entire movie?" I whispered to Tyler during a particularly funny scene. It was the movie we watched on our first date, and I remembered every detail.

"Like it was yesterday," he whispered back, squeezing my hand in reassurance.

The final credits rolled, a soft melody playing us out of the story we'd all been lost in. I hit the off button on the remote, and the screen faded to black, reflecting our still faces on its glassy surface. The boys were sprawled across one end of the couch, their eyelids heavy; the fight against sleep nearly won. Tyler's steady breathing brushed my cheek, his chest rising and falling in the rhythm that always soothed me.

"Best movie night ever," Max murmured, his words slurring into a yawn.

"Totally," Garrett mumbled in agreement, not far behind his brother in the journey to dreamland.

I smiled, the corners of my lips lifting with a weightlessness that had felt foreign for too long. The laughter from moments ago still hung in the air, a tangible reminder of the simplicity of joy. It was just... nice. No, more than that—it was perfect.

"Let's do it again next week," I suggested, already picturing another evening like this one: no shadows lurking, no whispers trailing.

"Definitely," Tyler said, his voice low and comforting. His eyes met mine, holding a promise that wasn't just about movie nights.

We sat there for a while longer, none of us making a move to break the spell of contentment. The room was dim, lit only by the faint glow of streetlamps filtering through the curtains. Crickets chirped outside a quiet soundtrack to our suburban life. Nothing else mattered right now—not the Winters, not the neighborhood chatter, not the uncertainties of tomorrow.

"Bedtime, guys," I finally said, though my heart tugged at the thought of disrupting this peace. "You can help clean up in the morning."

"Deal," they both sighed, too tired to protest or negotiate for a later bedtime.

As they shuffled off to their rooms, I lingered in the living room, taking in the remnants of our family time. The blankets were a tangled mess, popcorn kernels dotted the floor, and the cushions bore the imprints of our evening together. And it was beautiful.

"Coming?" Tyler's voice pulled me from my reverie.

"Yup, just a second," I answered, scanning the room once more, locking the memory in place.

I stood, turned off the lights, and followed the path of laughter echoes to our bedroom. Slipping beneath the cool sheets, I nestled close to Tyler, his warmth a solid presence in the night. Outside, the world kept spinning, but everything was still inside our little cocoon.

"Love you," I whispered, the words spilling out with the ease of truth.

"Love you more," he replied, a smile in his voice.

I closed my eyes, the day's images dancing behind my lids—bright flowers, laughing children, a house emptied of its secrets. This was what mattered: us, together, weathering whatever storms might come. With that thought cradling me, I drifted to sleep, my heart full, my mind at peace.

Grateful.

Thirteen

The soft glow of the TV bathed the living room in a pale light, flickering across our faces as we settled into the familiar dip of our well-worn couch. The kids were finally asleep, and we were about to watch the latest in our favorite show. It had become our Sunday evening ritual. Phones were off, no distractions: just my love and I.

"Pass the popcorn," I murmured without taking my eyes off the screen where the detective was inching closer to his big reveal. My husband obliged, the bowl shifting between us with a soft rustle of kernels. There was something about the crunch, the salt on my tongue, that just made everything feel right.

And then, without any warning, the scene cut abruptly to a stern-faced news anchor, her expression grim enough to make my heart skip. Living in a small town, they only do this if something big happens. "We interrupt this program with breaking news," she announced, and I felt that strange prickling sensation crawls up my spine.

"Hey, what the—" my husband started to grumble, but his voice trailed off as the anchor continued.

"Jetland Winters, local business tycoon known for his successful chain of tech stores, innovative computer applications, and security software, has been found dead." The words hit me like a physical blow, and for a moment, I couldn't breathe. Jetland—dead?

"What?" I whispered, my voice sounding hollow to my own ears.

My mind reeled. It didn't make sense. People like Jetland didn't just end up... dead.

"Oh shit..."

What about Billie? Was she... okay?

But the anchor was already answering my question. "Winters' body was discovered at a campsite in the early hours of the morning," she said, and for a second, the world seemed to pause on its axis. "His vehicle was seen entering the campground on Friday and then leaving the area shortly after midnight Saturday."

Noises around me—the ticking of our wall clock, the rattle of our dishwasher—faded into nothingness as I tried to reconcile the image of Jet, proud and controlling, with the silent, lifeless form they described. How could the man who demanded such order in life be swept away by such a chaotic end? Maybe he just... drowned. I wanted to know how. I needed to know what happened. But at the same time. I didn't. The details would only etch the tragedy deeper into reality, and part of me wanted to stay suspended in disbelief, where things could still be undone.

"Stella, honey?" My husband's hand found mine, squeezing gently. I turned to look at him, not really seeing. He was my rock, always. "Are you okay?"

"Sorry, just... processing," I managed to say, my voice a little steadier now. But inside, my thoughts were swirling. This didn't make sense.

They just moved. They were fixing things. That's why Billie ended our friendship.

But Jetland Winters was gone. And nothing would ever be the same again.

Images flickered on the screen. A recording of a house and a woman with a microphone standing in front announcing an arrest. I recognized that house. It was Billie's parents' house. In the background, tucked just barely in the frame, was Jet's truck, muddy and dirty, a bloody handprint smeared on the handle.

Oh my God...

She kept talking, but I couldn't make out the words. There she was—Billie—my friend whose laughter had filled these very walls, being paraded before the hungry press lenses. Her wrists were bound by cold steel, her head bowed, and her blonde hair shielding her face from view. But even from this angle, even with her gaze cast downwards, I could see it: fear mingling with resignation. The Billie I knew, who'd patch up skinned knees and offer hugs freely, looked so small against the backdrop of flashing lights and stern-faced officers. Her shirt was smeared with dried blood; her shoes were muddied. She must have panicked when she got home, not even thinking about what she'd done. Or how to get rid of the evidence.

She basically handed herself over to them.

The kids. Oh my God. Knowing she would be caught, she was probably saying goodbye to the kids.

"Billie..." I murmured, more to myself than anyone else, my breath catching in my throat as she lifted her head and stared straight into the video camera. The image of her haunted eyes seared into my mind, a stark contrast to the vibrant woman who once stood in my kitchen, sunlight dancing in her hair as we joked about the trials of parenthood.

My heart raced, pounding against my ribs as if trying to break free from the horror unfolding before us. The scene's gravity pulled at me, a vortex of disbelief and sorrow that threatened to swallow me whole.

The room suddenly felt like it was closing in, the walls inching closer with each dreadful word spilling from the TV. The feed cut back to the anchor as he continued talking. Speculating about what could have happened. "Prime suspect..." His voice boomed as if he were sitting right beside us, his tone grave, slicing through the silence that had cocooned us on our couch. I caught the tail end of what he was saying as I zoned back in. "Run over and left for dead..."

"Can you believe this?" I whispered, my voice a mere breath, disbelief clawing at my throat. It was Billie up there, her name now tangled in the twisted narrative of a crime so vile. Horror laced with incredulity knotted my stomach as I struggled to reconcile the image of her, handcuffed and broken, with the woman who'd been my friend.

"Baby..." My husband's voice, usually a balm, is now tight. I turned to look at him, his face etched with lines of concern.

In the dim glow of the television, shadows played across his features as he reached out, enveloping my hand in his. Warmth spread from his touch. His fingers intertwined with mine, a silent promise that I wasn't alone.

"Billie wouldn't... she couldn't..." The protest died on my lips, a feeble attempt to defend the friend I thought I knew. But the images kept coming—a still frame of her face behind the wheel of Jetland's truck, the accusation hanging heavy in the air between us.

"Hey," he squeezed my hand, grounding me as my mind threatened to spiral, "we don't know the whole story. Let's just... let's wait and see, okay?"

I didn't have the energy to respond, my eyes returning to the screen.

"Early Friday," the anchor's narration drilled into the silence, "Mrs. Winters had left her children at her parent's residence, reportedly for a weekend getaway with her husband."

"According to her mother, Mrs. Winters returned without her husband just after six a.m. the following morning. She called the police, allowing her daughter enough time to say goodbye to her children."

My heart thudded painfully against my ribcage, a crescendo of dread building as the anchor delivered the final blow. "Police arrested Mrs. Winters, and she is in custody pending charges. Please respect the privacy of her children at this time." The room closed in around me, pushing the air from my lungs.

The anchor's voice faded into a distant echo, the details of their investigation becoming white noise as I stared blankly. Tyler reached over, grabbed the remote from my hand, and clicked the TV off.

A heavy silence smothered the room, the kind that weighs on your chest and steals your breath. I looked at him, his eyes dark pools of worry.

"Stella..." he began, but words failed us both. What do you say when the world you thought you knew shatters? When someone you knew turned out to be someone you didn't?

My phone erupted into chaos of pings and vibrations, the sounds clashing against the stillness that had settled over us. I snatched it from the coffee table, and the screen was a blur of notifications—texts, missed calls, voicemails—all chiming in with urgency.

Is this for real? Billie?? One message read, the confusion palpable even through the text.

Stella, have you seen the news about Billie? What on earth happened? another friend asked, the words dripping with disbelief.

Call me ASAP, a neighbor said, her usual reserve lost to the shock-waves rippling through our little community.

Good riddance! The message came from Steve.

I scrolled through the messages, each one a hammer blow to the reality I thought I knew. These were people who lived on our street and who watched our kids play together. And now... now what?

"Can you believe this?" Tyler's voice was tight, his thumb hovering over his own device, no doubt besieged by similar cries of astonishment.

I shook my head, unable to form the words. My throat felt like sandpaper; my thoughts churned like a storm-tossed sea. How could this happen? What made her snap like this?

"Babe, talk to me," Tyler pulled me to his chest.

"Billie..." I finally whispered, the name tasting bitter, foreign. "She's not... she can't be capable of..."

But the images on the screen, the bloody shirt, the still of her driving his truck, the anchor's grave tone—they all painted a different portrait. My mind raced, trying to reconcile the two versions of my friend: the warm, anxious soul who'd confided her fears over cups of tea and the murderer led away in cuffs, despair etched into every feature.

"Maybe there's an explanation," I murmured, more to myself than to him. "There has to be."

"We don't really know everything. That is just what the reporter has said. There's gotta be more to the story," he said, but his eyes didn't hold the conviction his words tried to convey.

"More to the story," I echoed hollowly. Was there? Or had I been blind to a truth lurking beneath the surface, a darkness that she hid? After all, she had been so quick to throw me away. What's to say she didn't tire of Jet and threw him away, too? What if this whole time, it wasn't him who was abusive... it was her? The memory of her throwing a book at him flashed before my eyes. The plates. The text from Jet.

But another piece of me whispered, *what if... what if she snapped from the abuse and killed him?*

"Mom, why are you crying?" The small, concerned voice jolted me from my spiraling thoughts. Max stood in the hallway, rubbing sleep from his eyes.

"Nothing, sweetheart. It's just... grown-up stuff." I forced a smile, wiping away the traitorous tears that had escaped.

"Come here, son," my husband said, opening his arms to him. He ran to him, seeking the safety of his embrace, oblivious to the storm that had descended upon us.

"Did you have a nightmare?"

"Yeah... can you tuck me in?" Max's small voice was muffled against Tyler's shirt.

Tyler picked him up and kissed his forehead, walking down the hall and murmuring to him, "Of course I can."

I shivered, though the room wasn't cold. Something akin to acceptance washed over me. She'd pushed me away, snapped, and made her decisions. They were hers and hers alone. I'd made my peace. I'd moved on.

A chill of realization settled in the pit of my stomach, perhaps, that there were depths to every person that remained unseen, unknowable. What secrets had Billie kept? What had I overlooked?

My thoughts stilled as I mulled over the events that led us here. Maybe I wasn't meant to understand. Maybe the lesson in all of this is that we all have darkness, and we try to hide it, and it takes one defining moment to strip away the mask.

And then all the ugly on the inside comes pouring out.

Epilogue

One Year Later

I flipped through the stack of envelopes, mostly junk mail and bills. But then, my fingers stumbled upon something unexpected—a plain white envelope with no return address. The looping and familiar handwriting clenched my heart in an icy grip. It was Billie's. It had been a year since she killed Jet—a year of recovery and a return to normalcy. We'd even gotten news last week that I was finally pregnant and expecting our third. We were thrilled.

And just like that, my peace was shattered. I hadn't expected to ever hear from her again...

I hesitated momentarily; my breath caught in my throat before tearing it open. Inside was a single sheet of paper, the words scrawled passionately.

"Dear Stella," it began, and the world fell silent around me.

"I'm writing this because I can't bear the thought of you not knowing the truth—the whole sickening truth that's been eating at me.

You know about Jetland, but you don't know why. God, Stella, it was because of you."

My hands trembled, the letter quivering. I can almost hear the anxiety laced in her words, the vulnerability she always tried to hide.

"Remember when I left hints, small gestures, hoping you'd understand. I loved you, Stella, not just as a friend but as something fierce, burning, and terrifying. When I left Jetland, it wasn't for space; it was a desperate plea. I wanted you to see... to leave Tyler and be with me. Jetland was never the problem. I wanted you to save me. To run away with me. We could have had it all, started again, started new."

I slumped against the counter. She loved me? What? All she ever talked about was... how much she wanted to get away from him.

Oh my God. How did I miss this?

I forced myself to continue reading, each sentence a shard of ice sliding beneath my skin. "You didn't see it, did you? My rage boiled over when I realized that my love for you was invisible. Like whispers in a hurricane, gone unheard." The paper crackled as my grip tightened. "I became something dark, something twisted. I destroyed your property—the flower garden you'd planted with Tyler. I learned how to hack cameras, ensuring you wouldn't be able to see for weeks. I even left a little hint that it was me—a piece of my ribbon hidden in the dirt.

I bet you never found it. That night, you almost caught me; all I was trying to do was look into your room to see what HE gets to experience night after night—the way your body molds around him. I wanted to be him, even if just for a moment. I'd been doing it for months already. Just... peeking through that small sliver of your window where the moon hits your mirror just right, and I could see you. I didn't expect the rage that followed. I'd already destroyed part of Jet's truck months ago in a fit of rage. Remember the night you and Tyler celebrated your tenth anniversary? Jett tried to be cute and invited me to make out with him in his truck in the field. I got pissed and smashed the side mirror. That rage was just the start.

Jetland... I tried, Stella. I tried to make it work with him again. But every time he touched me, I recoiled inside. Every 'I love you' he said... I felt nothing. He constantly reminded me of everything I couldn't have—of you. I don't know when it started. It was just... there one day. The kiss we shared made it worse. It was a burning under my skin. An itch I couldn't scratch. When you asked me if I was okay, I truly was. Until I wasn't. I kept waiting, and waiting, and waiting for you to leave Tyler. To come to me. I tried filling the hole with Steve, and for a while, it worked. But it wasn't enough. Nothing was. Nothing is. After we put the house for sale and went touring the country, things were fine for a bit, but I couldn't touch him. I couldn't do my duty as a wife, much less look at him as someone I could love the way I love you.

We went camping, hoping to rekindle something, anything. But there was nothing left. We argued. I told him I wanted a divorce. I wanted to leave, but he screamed at me. They told me I was a bitch for breaking our family apart. And then... it happened. A push, a fall, his head cracked against a rock. I watched the blood spill, and I felt nothing but relief. His hand came up. He tried to grab the handle to get up, but I pushed him down."

My heart hammered against my ribs, threatening to break free. "I didn't stop there. I climbed into his truck and drove over him. Once, twice—ensuring my freedom. I didn't really think much past that, as you can tell. I don't regret it, Stella. Not for a second. I'd do it again, even though I told them I wouldn't. It's funny what you can get away with if you just tell them you're depressed and aren't doing well in the head.

And I'm furious at you, too. Furious that you never understood how much I love you, how much I want you. I'll be out in 18 months, thanks to good behavior. Can you believe it? Me, rewarded for playing nice. But when I'm out, I'll find you. We're meant to be together, Stella. You'll see. We will be together, babe. You and me. Forever.

xoxo,

Bills"

The letter slipped from my numb fingers, dancing to the floor in a slow waltz of horror. A chill crawled through me, one that seeped into my bones. Each word is etched into my mind, a haunting litany of obsession and madness.

Flabbergasted didn't even begin to cover what I felt. I remembered the kiss—a fleeting moment that I had cast aside as a fracture in time, a lapse in judgment fueled by too much wine and too little sleep. But it was more, wasn't it? It was Billie laying her heart bare, and I had been too blind to see it.

The breakup with Jetland and the endless texts that filled my phone's memory cascaded through my mind now with painful clarity. Each message is a cry for attention, a plea wrapped in casual conversation. And her attitude—the way her warmth would vanish into cold frustration when I left her waiting for a reply. It all made sense, a puzzle finally pieced together in the most horrific of pictures.

She never hated me.

She'd been in love with me.

I heard the front door close and the familiar sound of keys clinking against the wooden entryway table. Tyler was home.

"Tyler," I called out, my voice a ghost of its usual confidence.

He rounded the corner, eyes scanning my face with that intuitive concern of his. "Babe? What's wrong?"

"We need to move," the words launched from my lips. "We can't stay here."

"Move? Stella, what are you talking about?" His brows knitted together in confusion.

"Read this," I bent down, grabbed the letter, and pushed the paper toward him with a shaky hand. "It's from Billie."

As he unfolded the creases and scanned the handwriting I knew so well, his face changed from curiosity to disbelief. Slowly, he put the letter on the table.

Tyler looked up, his expression unreadable, his face drained of all color. "Stella..."

"Eighteen months, Ty." My voice was a whisper of dread. "We have eighteen months to disappear."

Dear Stella,

I'm writing this because I can't bear the thought of you not knowing the truth —the whole sickening truth that's been eating at me. You know about Jetland, but you don't know why. God, Stella, it was because of you. Remember the times I left hints, small gestures, hoping you'd understand? I loved you, Stella, not just as a friend but as something fierce, burning, and terrifying. When I left Jetland, it wasn't for space; it was a desperate plea. I wanted you to see... to leave Tyler and be with me. Jetland was never the problem. I wanted you to save me. To run away with me. We could have had it all, started again, started new.

You didn't see it, did you? My rage boiled over when I realized that my love for you was invisible. Like whispers in a hurricane, gone unheard." The paper crackled as my grips tightened. "I became something dark, something twisted. I destroyed your property—the flower garden you'd planted with Tyler. I learned how to hack cameras, ensuring you wouldn't be able to see for weeks. I even left a little hint that it was me—a piece of my ribbon hidden in the dirt. I bet you never found it. That night, you almost caught me; all I was trying to do was look into your room to see what H.C. gets to experience night after night—the way your body molds around him. I wanted to be him, even if just for a moment. I'd been doing it for months already. Just... peeking through that small sliver of your window where the moon hits your mirror just right, and I could see you. I didn't expect the rage that followed. I'd already destroyed part of Jet's truck months ago in a fit of rage. Remember the night you and Tyler celebrated your tenth anniversary? Jett tried to be cute and invited me to make out with him in his truck in the field. I got pissed and smashed the side mirror. That rage was just the start.

Jetland... I tried, Stella. I tried to make it work with him again. But every time he touched me, I recoiled inside. Every "I love you" he said... I felt nothing. He constantly reminded me of everything I couldn't have—of you. I don't know when it started. It was just... there one day. The kiss we shared made it worse. It was a burning under my skin. An itch I couldn't scratch. When you asked me if I was okay, I truly was. Until I wasn't. I kept waiting, and waiting, and waiting for you to leave Tyler. To come to me. I tried filling the hole with Steve, and for a while, it worked. But it wasn't enough. Nothing was. Nothing is. After we put the house for sale and went touring the country, things were fine for a bit, but I couldn't touch him. I couldn't do my duty as a wife, much less look at him as someone I could love the way I love you.

We went camping, hoping to rekindle something, anything. But there was nothing left. We argued. I told him I wanted a divorce. I wanted to leave, but he screamed at me. They told me I was a bitch for breaking our family apart. And then... it happened. A push, a fall, his head cracked against a rock. I watched the blood spill, and I felt nothing but relief. His hand came up. He tried to grab the handle to get up, but I pushed him down.

I didn't stop there. I climbed into his truck and drove over him. Once, twice—ensuring my freedom. I didn't really think much past that, as you can tell. I don't regret it, Stella. Not for a second. I'd do it again, even though I told them I wouldn't. It's funny what you can get away with if you just tell them you're depressed and aren't doing well in the head.

And I'm furious at you, too. Furious that you never understood how much I love you, how much I want you. I'll be out in 18 months, thanks to good behavior. Can you believe it? Me, rewarded for playing nice. But when I'm out, I'll find you. We're meant to be together, Stella. You'll see. We will be together, babe. You and me. Forever.

xoxo,

Billy

Also By

Find all of Stephanie's works here
To find out what happens next, click here

About

Stephanie writes across genres. She lives with her spouse out in the country. She has chickens and cats and is passionate about all things flowers, food, bees, and trees.

All her romance is written under Stephanie Swann and you'll find her non-romance under S.L Swann.

Join Stephanie's newsletter for freebies, updates, and discounts! https://thedopaminedemon.myflodesk.com

***

You can contact Stephanie at: stephanieswann.author@gmail.com

Instagram: authorstephanieswann
Facebook: Stephanie Swann
Tiktok: stephanieswannauthor
Other Links: https://linktr.ee/stephanieswannauthor

Acknowledgements

For my Ride or Die: you've kept me sane when I otherwise wouldn't be. Sisterhood for life.

For my Best Whore: thanks for being you. 17 years strong and many, many more to go. I love you through it all.

For the Parent Group: I appreciate you all being there, in the worst of times, and in the best.

For my Love You Long Time: may we one day strike it rich so we can build a commune. Love you long time. Thank you for being my sanity in this extremely upside down, curvy, confusing landscape, for listening to my rants and allowing me to be free. Thank you for giving me the courage to just be me.

For the Otherworldly Obsessions: I hope we go semi-viral, but not too viral, so we can continue being as unhinged as we are, while writing our books and supporting each other in the very best of ways. You ladies have loved and accepted me in this cutthroat world and I love and appreciate you all so much.

For my Twisted Sister, who wrote a book that I fell in love with and then fangirled over enough that I ended up messaging you and we became fast friends, I have so much love for you. I hope we continue to breast boobily and send each other weird chin pics until the day we die.

For my Dopamine Demons, you are all such amazing people. Thank you for standing in my corner while I've struggled, while I've thrived. Thank you for allowing me to vent, to cry, to survive. Thank you for sharing your lives with me. Thank you for trusting me to build worlds that you want to read, characters that you relate to. Thank you for being there for me. I don't know where I'd be without you. Thank you for giving me a chance. I love you all.

Made in the USA
Coppell, TX
21 September 2024